£3.00 DH WK
48

ERMINIA DELL'ORO (Asmara, 1938) is the granddaughter of one of the first Italian settlers who arrived in Eritrea in 1886. At the age of twenty she moved to Milan to continue her studies. She visited Asmara, where her family lived, to write articles and reports. Her first book, *Asmara Addio* (1988) was a great success. She is the author of many books both for adults and children. Currently, Erminia is involved in promoting reading and participates in meetings in various regions of Italy in schools, libraries and prisons.

OONAGH STRANSKY has translated book-length works by Montale, Lucarelli, Pontiggia and Saviano as well as short stories and essays by Spaziani, Pasolini, Stassi, Pericoli and D'Eramo. Her translation of Starnone's *The House on Via Gemito* (Europa 2023) was longlisted for the International Booker Prize and was shortlisted for the Oxford-Weidenfeld Prize. Born in Paris and raised in the Middle East, London and the United States, Oonagh studied Italian at Middlebury College, UC Berkeley, the Università di Firenze and Columbia University. She now resides in Italy.

ERMINIA DELL'ORO

Abandonment

*Translated from the Italian
by Oonagh Stransky*

HÉLOÏSE
PRESS

First published in English in Great Britain in 2024 by
Héloïse Press Ltd
4 Pretoria Road
Canterbury CT1 1QL
www.heloisepress.com

L'abbandono: una storia Eritrea © Erminia Dell'Oro 2024,
first published by Einaudi, Italy, in 1991.

This translation © Oonagh Stransky 2024

Cover design by Laura Kloos
Edited by Ruth Clarke

Text design and typesetting by Tetragon, London
Printed and bound in Great Britain by CPI Group (UK) Ltd, Croydon, CR0 4YY

The moral right of Erminia Dell'Oro to be identified as the author of this work has been asserted in accordance with the Copyrights, Designs and Patents Act, 1988.

Oonagh Stransky asserts her moral right to be identified as the translator of the work.

All rights reserved. Except as otherwise permitted under current legislation, no part of this publication may be reproduced or transmitted in any form or by any means, electronic or mechanical, including photocopy, recording, or any information storage and retrieval system, without permission in writing from the publisher.

This book has been selected to receive financial assistance from English PEN's PEN Translates programme, supported by Arts Council England. English PEN exists to promote literature and our understanding of it, to uphold writers' freedoms around the world, to campaign against the persecution and imprisonment of writers for stating their views, and to promote the friendly co-operation of writers and the free exchange of ideas. www.englishpen.org

This book has been translated thanks to a translation grant awarded by the Italian Ministry of Foreign Affairs and International Cooperation.

Questo libro è stato tradotto grazie a un contributo alla traduzione assegnato dal Ministero degli Affari Esteri e della Cooperazione Internazionale italiano.

ISBN 978-1-7384594-0-7

To the free people of Eritrea

1

When the universe lit up its suns and stars in infinite space, it trembled momentarily with magic, then understood that it was alone and always would be, so it cried. A host of angels flew across the skies, the light dappling their wings with colour, and disappeared. The universe sighed heavily, its tears crystallising into alternate worlds that preserved the dream, or memory, of those luminous wings. Now when the cosmos recalls its ancient suffering and the trail of colours that gently caressed it to lessen the pain, a rainbow appears in the sky.

After the final rains of the year, such a bridge of light appeared above Adi Ugri, a village in the Eritrean highlands. Sellass took it as a sign from God that it was time to tell her five sisters and one brother that she wanted to leave. Each day in that wretched land was a gamble with life; she did not want to raise children in a place where she had experienced so much suffering. Her parents were dead and her sisters and brother managed to survive by working arid patches of land with their families.

Sellass was twelve years old. If she stayed, she would have to get married and accept a future devoid of hope.

When Tecle, a distant cousin, came back to Adi Ugri for a few days, he told her about the big body of water that was the sea and the white city called Massawa. Tecle had learnt a profession there and would only return to the highlands to die.

Sellass' family approved of her decision. She was an adult now and they had enough troubles without her becoming yet another.

'Never serve the white man,' Mebrat, the eldest of her sisters, told her. 'This is our country. We must never be their servants.'

Alefesc, a much-loved aunt, gave Sellass plenty of advice and an amulet to protect her from the evil eye.

'You are too beautiful, Sellass,' she said, embracing her. 'Be careful that your beauty does not lead to disgrace.'

Alefesc told stories better than anyone, enchanting Sellass. She called forth the spirits of the air and filled the evening hours with magical figures. She spoke in the voices of the dead, first as an old man and then as a child, and Sellass would lose herself in the tales.

Sometimes Alefesc disappeared like one of the spirits and vanished into the hidden blue canyons of the sky. People in town said that the demon Zar came to possess her and carried her off, screaming, into the mountains.

When Sellass woke up in the dark of night and heard Alefesc shrieking, she would cover her ears with her hands and call out to God, hoping to frighten away the demons that drove Alefesc into a frenzy.

At times like that, even the hyenas ran off. All voices ceased. Madness, the greatest fear of all humans, left even the shadows short of breath.

Sellass tied the amulet around her neck, bundled up her few things, said goodbye to everyone, kissed the hand and robe of the village *cascì*, and began her descent towards the sea. To feel less lonely on her journey, she daydreamed and sang. God had created a bridge that would carry her far from her village, she was crossing the sky, and the spirits of the air travelled silently by her side to keep away fear.

When the sun suddenly went down and the shadows of night appeared, darkening those immense spaces, Sellass felt terror grip her heart like a vice. It was as if the many voices of obscurity were tiptoeing across her clothes and face, each one a breath of terror.

She closed her eyes and summoned the benign spirits of the night, asking them to distance the jackals and hyenas that howled at the moon. But her heart continued to pound in her chest, and when she saw the cone-shaped roof of a tukul in the shadows, she asked the family who lived there to host her until dawn.

She took up her journey again before the sun had fully risen and, a few hours later, she saw before her the parched and fiery expanse of the lowlands.

She encountered a caravan of Rashaida merchants, with veiled women bobbing about on camels, causing their heavy earrings to jangle. Their proud and remote manner made them seem like creatures of her imagination. One of the merchants asked which direction she was travelling and invited her to ride on a camel through the desert. They were going to the sea too, he said, but not to Massawa. They were going somewhere else, much farther away.

When Sellass went back to walking alone, she started to fear the heat, the way it made her head spin and tongue swell.

Her long dress was soaked with sweat and her bundle weighed heavily on her shoulders. She tried to resist drinking the little water she had left until she knew how far it was to the sea.

She came upon a group of men and women sorrowfully dragging themselves along towards Massawa. The effort had drained them entirely; they wore the desperate expressions of people who were following a last, disappearing glimmer of life. They were like the dying, who see a flicker of light, invisible to everyone else, that keeps them alive. It was as if the scorching desert had had a nightmare and they were the result. It occurred to Sellass that if she joined them, she would surely die. This only made her heart pound harder. She overtook them: none of those desperate souls even noticed her.

When she reached Otumlo, a vast expanse of desert just outside the city gates, the sun was setting. The hot air was heavy with an unbearable odour, and here and there she saw shapes that reminded her of the ghost worlds described by her aunt Alefesc.

Sellass had always lived in poverty. She knew what hunger, epidemics, fatigue and death were.

She had seen young people and children die. She had grown accustomed to the despair that resided in her village.

But now, close to collapse from heat, thirst and weariness, when she looked at the remains of those men and women, she felt her chest fill with devastating agony.

Crawling across the hot sand of the plains of Otumlo like dark insects were the sick and infected, either pursuing a sudden hallucination that beckoned to them from the desert of death or trying to get away from other people, in order to protect, as well as possible and in extreme solitude, a desperate sense of modesty.

Withered, toothless women pointed at immobile babies that stared at the sky. Cadavers lay abandoned to insects. Jackals howled in the distance.

Sellass approached a young woman who was making her way from one shadowy figure to the next, leaning over them, while they reached their skeletal arms up towards her.

'Where are we?' Sellass tried to ask, but her voice failed her.

'The plains of Otumlo,' the woman said. 'These people were chased out of Massawa because they are sick. I came here to find a leprous woman from my village. I promised I would try and help her, they told me she was brought here.' The woman looked at Sellass. 'Get away from here. Go.'

Sellass saw a group of children fighting over a donkey's innards, the carcass swarming with insects. Vultures screamed and swooped down towards them.

Then, passing in the distance, she saw a caravan. The camels were headed towards the sea and the caravan drivers seemed intent on ignoring the outcasts of Otumlo. Sellass could see the opulent dresses of the women sitting astride the animals and the white fabric of the men's turbans. Barefoot children walked behind them, carrying flaming torches.

Sellass was tempted to run to them and ask them to take her with them but she did not have the strength to take another step. Besides, she thought, they'd probably think she was one of the sick people.

An old man with a long, thick white beard led a lamb over to a squatting woman.

'Your son is dead,' he said, offering the animal to the woman. 'Nurse the lamb and fatten it up, so we can feed it to the weakest.'

The woman brought the bleating lamb to her breast. On the ground, by her side, lay an infant wrapped in a shroud. The woman had woven the cloth in her village and brought it with her on their long journey so that if death came to them, her son would not go naked to the earth.

Sellass felt as though she was carrying all the suffering of the world on her shoulders and in her heart; the world was nothing more than that desert of desperation filled with faces disfigured by hunger, people who refused to succumb to death wearing expressions of terror, wailing men and women marked by profound humiliation.

She looked at the sky, which the last rays of sun had washed with red and gold, and in its vast beauty, which was so very indifferent to the pain that dwelt in the desert, she sought a sign of salvation, a prayer to help her leave that place.

She thought of the highlands, of Adi Ugri, and she remembered the rainbow. God had not brought her this far to die. She dried her tears and drank the water that remained.

'Is it far to Massawa?' she asked the old man with the white beard.

'It's over there,' he said, extending his arm. 'A few minutes' walk and you'll be able to smell the sea.'

2

The colours of the sea were iridescent. In the distance sat the island of Sheik Said, a green dot on the violet and azure waters. Massawa, which was built on a block of mother-of-pearl that rose up out of the waves, had long been one of the most important ports in the Red Sea.

During the years when Mussolini had been intent on building a colonial empire, Massawa was a bustling city. Muslims, Jews, Indians and Greeks devoted themselves to their businesses. Teams of Eritreans laboured alongside Italians on the construction of railways, roads and buildings.

In various spots around town, old local women would squat on the ground and set up improvised markets, hawking their *mangerie*, a word they invented to describe the small piles of spices and grains, buzzing with flies, that they spread out on crumpled pieces of paper.

During the scorching hours of the day, when even the wild dogs slunk off to look for shade, fat and sweaty Arab men sat at the *teccerie* smoking their *scibuk*, revelling in both the smoke and the lazy feeling that came over them.

Young black children spent their days on the streets.

They came out of their hidden, smelly, rat-infested alleyways in the morning, bringing swarms of faithful flies with them, and returned there together at day's end to sleep. Despite being gaunt and malnourished, the children always found the strength to come up with new and inventive ways of scrounging together a few pennies.

In the gaps between hunting for their means of survival, they played with coloured pebbles, often arguing and even fighting over them. Their disputes would go on until a *zeptié* guard came along with his kurbash: the whip would crack loudly and, as if a magic spell had transformed them into lizards, the children would vanish into dark corners.

A few minutes later they would reappear, looking for their scattered pebbles. If one of them suddenly ran off, the others would follow, a signal that a possible benefactor was nearby. They would then hunt down and surround this person, reach out their tiny hands and overwhelm their victim with a litany of beseeching voices. And when the passing donor pulled out some change, always grumbling that this would be the last time, the little beggar children would kick and push each other, never losing sight of the hand, trying to grab the money without thinking about dividing it fairly. Once the moment of greed had passed, which usually coincided with the arrival of the guard and his trusty kurbash, the little ones would disappear, as if swallowed up by nothingness. Back in their shadowy corners, they calmly and peacefully split up the coins before returning to the streets. This went on until night swallowed them up again.

In the evening, the lights of Massawa illuminated the sea with reflections that followed the movement of the waves; the city was calm in a way that it could not be during the day.

Government officials came out to stroll in their elegant uniforms. Labourers, weary after their long days of work, wandered up and down the streets, chatting among themselves and glancing at the teccerie where Eritrean ladies, dressed in loud colours, waited for occasional company.

Sellass quickly grew accustomed to the noisy and vibrant city. She forgot Otumlo. It felt like that stretch of land, the desperation and death, had been a terrible dream that her mind had erased. Her twelve-year-old self looked with cheer and optimism at the city she had managed to reach.

She immediately found accommodation with a kind Eritrean family in the neighbourhood of Taulud in exchange for carrying water from one side of the city to the other every day. Everybody liked Sellass: she was pretty, cheerful and kind; her radiant smile made her very attractive. She was skinny but strong as she had not known any serious illnesses in her native village, where children constantly died like flowers cut down by the wind.

Sellass sang while she transported water and the city soon became familiar to her; it was as if she had always lived there. She often sat with the women who sold mangerie, helping them form piles of dura and teff, and talking about her distant village. She sat on the ground and watched the passing traffic, she saw large ships full of men and merchandise come and go from the port, she heard languages she did not know, always trying to pick up a word here and there.

Towards evening, she would go and sit with Mariam, the cripple.

Mariam spent her days in a shady corner near the Governor's Palace. No one dared send Mariam out to the plains of Otumlo or any other forgotten part of the world because she commanded both fear and respect. Mariam always carried her shells with her; she used them to read the passage of time, whispering people's futures to them, interweaving them with the mystery that kept them concealed. They said that Mariam had always been there and that she knew everyone's secrets, as if thousands of voices travelled through the air to sit at her twisted feet and tell their tales. They even said that shades from the kingdom of death came to her at night – transported by the waves, whispering magical fables – only to dissolve with the first light of day.

Mariam kept her face partially covered with a faded, hand-woven futah; only her bright kohl-lined eyes were visible, and they took in every worldly thing around her.

Sellass listened to Mariam's stories and let herself be drawn into the mysterious universe of the crippled woman with both fear and enchantment.

'Mariam, read me my shells,' Sellass said one day, sitting on the ground next to her. She had asked her many other times, but the woman was not always willing to look into the future with the handful of small seashells that she kept in a bowl by her side.

Mariam sat in silence for a few minutes, transferring the tiny objects from one hand to the other, before letting them fall to the ground.

Sellass looked at them and tried to understand the secret, but all she saw were small, shiny shells, dotted with grey and pink.

'A man will come from across the sea,' Mariam said, 'and you will be his woman.'

Sellass stared harder at the shells.

'I will never serve the white people,' she said. 'This is our country and we must never serve them.'

'You will be his woman,' Mariam repeated. 'Not his servant.' She gathered up the shells, shook them in her cupped hands and let them fall again. 'Your brother serves the white man,' she said. 'And then I see him disappear.'

'Will I be happy?' Sellass asked anxiously.

'That,' Mariam replied, putting the shells back in the bowl, 'I cannot say. After the man, I see only fog. But today I am tired and the shells do not respond the way I would like.'

'Mariam.' A fat Arab man in a long white djellaba stopped in front of the two women. 'Tell me when Sellass will sleep with me, and tell her that I will cover her with gold.'

Sellass got to her feet, picked up the waterskins that she had leaned against the wall, and slung them over her shoulders. 'Lots of *sciarmutte* would be happy to have your *talleri*, Ahmed,' she said, embraced Mariam and walked away.

The Arab man watched her, jingling his coins in his pocket.

'She will never sleep with you,' Mariam said. 'There are other men for a girl like Sellass.'

'Of course there are,' Ahmed replied. 'White men want girls just like her. They'll end up becoming their sciarmutte, and soon our country will be filled with bastard children. Even the high and mighty governor would gladly have a beauty like Sellass, if he could.' He kicked over Mariam's bowl of shells and coins. 'As for you, old loaf,' he added, spitting on the ground, 'convince her with those shells of yours to come with me, or I'll have you kicked out of here.'

'Sellass,' Mariam replied calmly, 'will never go with you. Look elsewhere, Ahmed. And if you do anything against me – I, who only have this corner to live in – you will never know peace again.'

The Arab threw a coin at her feet, as if to be forgiven for threatening her and to ward off any potential bad luck. Then he set out towards the hidden alleys of Massawa, where, in front of dark and decrepit dwellings that smelled of mildew, Berbere spices and Abyssinian butter, semi-naked women lay on angarebs, forced by their hunger to sell pleasure.

3

At the age of twelve, Carlo Cinzi decided to leave his small town near Pavia and emigrate to America. He was the oldest of five boys. His parents farmed a small patch of land that never produced enough to feed the entire family; often, his father was forced to work as a day labourer on the estate of a rich gentleman.

Winters were long, and Carlo's mother, a slender and pale woman with a persistent cough, struggled to put aside all the wood and potatoes they needed to make it through the cold season. At night, her sisters and their children came over and they all sat near the big woodburning stove, the women knitting socks, the children playing with dolls, the youngest ones falling asleep on the floor with their heads resting on the hems of their mothers' long skirts. Carlo's mother spoke little; words sat like weights in her slight chest. She lived in a world of long silences and distant thoughts. Her husband understood this, or maybe he just accepted it. He talked to her rarely but showed his affection for her in ways that she was able to intuit.

Usually Carlo's father went to bed early, but on Saturdays he stayed out late. He said he went to the bar in town to have a drink with Gigi and his friends, to play cards. On Sundays he enjoyed spending time with the children or playing his recorder, which he kept safely hidden away from inexpert and tiny hands. In those rare moments, his large blue eyes lit up with happiness: the magic of music cheered up the room and the children gathered around, wishing they, too, could play the enchanted instrument and make music fly up into the air. In moments like that, his wife sat placidly with her knitting, gently tapping her feet to the rhythm.

One evening Carlo's father spoke of America.

'Aldo is happy there,' he said. 'He says there's lots of work. He sent money to Maria, and now his brother is going too.'

His wife stopped in front of the window, tracing her finger across the foggy glass.

'America is far,' she said, 'We don't know what's out there. Our home is here.'

'A home filled with hardship,' he said with a sigh, and the subject of America was never brought up again.

But Carlo continued to think about America. He talked to Aldo's brother about the vast country and asked him endless questions. Eventually he decided to undertake the journey to the great city on the sea, where there was employment for all. He started working as a day labourer to save up for the trip. One day he told his father that he wanted to join Aldo and learn a trade. He'd tell his mother later, he said; she had been ill for some time, she was weak and only got up from bed for a couple of hours each day.

His mother died without learning of her son's plans. The image of that sad day would remain imprinted in Carlo's memory: people walking in and out of the dark bedroom, the candles slowly going out, women crying – the poor thing, they said, she wore out her lungs, now who will take care of the children? Her husband sat in the corner with a lost air. He had known that his wife was very ill but death was a sad thought that he had always kept at a distance.

An aunt came to live with them, a shapely woman who wore her hair pulled back in bright kerchiefs. In a relatively short time, Carlo's father's mood improved. He even stayed at home on Saturday evenings to play his recorder; the woman would sit in the corner and ask him to play this or that pretty tune she had heard at the fair, but he always ignored her and played whatever he wanted. The woman knew about Carlo's plan to travel to America and she told him it was a good idea that he go and seek his fortune, that he'd never find it in Italy, just as his father had never found his by toiling his whole life over a few clods of earth.

One day in May, Carlo packed a few things into a cardboard valise and got ready to leave. His siblings embraced him, pleased by the promise that Carlo had made them: that one day he would return and bring them all to the faraway land. Rita, his former schoolteacher, who had given him gifts of various kinds ever since his mother died – chestnuts, warm socks, even sweets that she had bought at a fair once – sent him off with a great deal of advice and two books, in which she had written dedications. One was an atlas that he instantly adored and the other was an old book of fables with illustrations of princes and wizards.

On his long voyage across the sea, Carlo spent a great deal of time looking out at the immense expanse of water and the seagulls; with their loud calls and swooping flights, they were the only beings that alleviated the solitude in which the ship seemed to be lost. Carlo felt silence penetrate deep into his soul, isolating him from the inhabited world, making him feel like an outsider. He dug into his memory for images that spoke to him and – appearing on the great waters of the ocean – he saw the shape of his river, the friends he used to play with on summer evenings, the fish that darted between their legs, how they skipped stones across the waves, the laughter and splashing; he heard the notes of a recorder and saw his mother bending down to light the fire.

In a short amount of time, Carlo managed to carve out a small space for himself in New York. Although he spoke little and always felt slightly alienated from life around him, he gave it his all; he understood immediately that the only way to survive in that city was to work hard. For a few years he helped out in the kitchen of a large restaurant, assisting the chefs and also learning to cook. Eventually, he was hired in a trattoria where the waiters were all Italian, but then came the crash of '29, the owner of the trattoria went out of business, and Carlo lost his job. The mood of the city plummeted, people were filled with worries and fear, and Carlo decided to return to Italy.

He had never managed to truly love New York; he had always felt like a shadow there, slipping noiselessly along the streets, getting trampled on with the indifference reserved for weightless and voiceless shapes.

His only friend had been Wolf, a black boy from Harlem. Wolf loved to talk, tell stories and sing beautiful songs, which held Carlo spellbound.

Together they had explored all the different neighbourhoods of the city, discovering their hidden secrets, but not even this had made Carlo like New York any better. In his friendship with Wolf, Carlo had found an ally to share their common destiny: they were both isolated from a world that was inaccessible to them.

On returning to his village, Carlo found the same poverty he had experienced as a child. His father was older and wearier, his aunt was fatter and no longer cheerful, his brothers had become men and all worked in the fields. He realised that his return had let them down; he had not made his fortune as he had promised.

'There's poverty there too,' Carlo said to explain why he had abandoned his old hopes. 'There's the Depression, everyone's scared, there might even be war.' Carlo had always been afraid of war. He never forgot how his grandfather never returned from the mountains where he had been sent to fight. His own father had spent months of his life on the run and in hiding. As a child, Carlo had often heard stories about the cruel enemy, the wounded, and the dead.

Carlo unwillingly went back to working the land. It felt like the townspeople scorned him: he was the same poor old sod he had always been.

When the Africa campaign was announced, Carlo decided to try his hand at adventure once again. Mussolini wanted to build a colonial empire and promised employment and wellbeing for all. Apparently they were investing millions. Il Duce said that over there, where the sun shone all year long, there was room for a great many Italians; they needed to construct new buildings in a hurry so that the empire could expand.

Ships departed from Italy laden with piles of cement and building materials, the ports were buzzing with excitement as if on the eve of a historic event, and men destined for great adventures headed towards the distant lands of Africa.

Carlo had moments of intense doubt before deciding to leave. It felt like he was leaving for war, that this time he was abandoning his town forever. He worried that he was getting involved in a tragedy that would unfold in a place too far away to even imagine. But then memories, thoughts and sensations of Wolf came flooding back to him. He recalled the tales his friend had sung while they walked around the harbour and up and down the avenues of New York. His songs had spoken of a return to a distant past, to an Africa of legends and magic, and they had always made him think of the continent where Wolf had his origins. Gradually, Carlo's doubts disappeared. There was simply too much poverty around him. He was glad to have the opportunity to leave again.

Carlo's father accompanied him to Genoa; he looked like a sad, old child, mystified by all the movement in the harbour, by the exclamations of farewell and the unintelligible shouting from the dock workers and sailors.

The voyage was very different from the one Carlo had taken years before. When he caught sight of the infinite horizon from the main deck, he felt a strange sensation come over him and was deeply moved. It was as if he realised, in that very moment, that he was experiencing the unrepeatable and marvellous adventure that is life; as if, for the first time, life itself – with its variety of colours and sounds and in the warm soothing sensation of the sun on his skin – was mysteriously promising him happiness.

4

The waves rose up high, grazed the clouds, then came crashing back down on Massawa, washing it all away. The island of Sheik Said, with its mangroves and white sand, shone in the sky and then it also disappeared. Even Sellass was lifted up by the wave, so high it felt like she could touch the sun, and then carried down deep to the tangle of coral branches and seashells.

'Sellass, Sellass,' the sea whispered, loosening her hair, removing her white dress and slipping off her bracelets. 'Sellass, Sellass,' it said, her name resounding through the depths like an echo, the water caressing her body.

The sea decorated her hair with shells, brought her red coral flowers and gave her the gift of a pearl that shone like an underwater sun.

Suddenly, Sellass felt a sharp pain in her chest: the quill of a sea urchin had pierced her heart. The urchin had snuck away from its master to punish the intruder who had enchanted the sea. Sellass felt life slipping away from her, she saw the white city resting at the bottom of the abyss, with Mariam sitting in a shadowy corner, scooping up her shells.

She tried to call out but had no voice, it had abandoned her.

'Sellass, Sellass,' the water whispered, the vivid fish swimming over to see the girl who had been loved by the sea, her long black hair turning into seaweed around her.

Then Sellass felt a deep languor come over her and she understood that her body was dissolving into the seawater, that the wave she had become was returning towards the light and slowly breaking on a beach where the shades of the dead had gathered. Even Mariam's shells were there, specks of darkness on the sand, and a hand reached out to grab them. The wave tried to speak, to say she was Sellass, but the voice was only a watery gurgle, and the shades, going through the gestures of life, ignored the coming and going of the wave.

Sellass shared her dream with Mariam, who once again told her that she would soon meet the man of her life, then about the long-ago earthquake that had destroyed Massawa, and finally about her own sister, whom the sea had dragged away. Sellass spent the day walking around town, stopping to talk to the women who sold mangerie, to the old Muslim tailor, who had promised her a new dress in exchange for bringing him water, and to Raissa, the woman in the tecceria near the port who drove the white men crazy with love, they said. Raissa wore see-through red dresses and piled her voluminous black hair high on her head like a crown; she painted her beautiful mouth vermilion and loved to laugh and joke. She knew all of Massawa's secrets, there were always people in her tecceria after the hottest hours had passed, and everyone sighed when they looked at her. They said that at night she slept with a rich white man who lived in the Governor's

Palace; he was the one who had given her the gold bracelets that jangled when she walked. He was also the one who sent a boy to scour the city for her when she suddenly fell prey to a new lover and disappeared into the warm night, leaving the scent of skin and crushed flowers behind her in the tecceria.

Sellass made her way to the lighthouse, where there was always a refreshing breeze; she enjoyed feeling the spray from the waves splash her face and clothes. A few children caught sight of her and ran up to her. The street children of Massawa adored Sellass and often followed her, just to hear her singing, because Sellass always sang when she walked, even when her waterskins were full and heavy. The children would giggle and touch her dress and then run off, she would pretend to be angry and say she did not enjoy that game, that she did not want them to touch her, and then she would go back to singing. Sometimes they sat down together on the ground in the shade, and she would pull a little something out of a knotted rag bundle for them. If the children started to bicker about who would be the first to receive a handful of seeds to crack open with their teeth, Sellass would threaten not to give any of them anything, and they would stop. Afterwards, they would play with multicoloured pebbles, rolling them across the hot cobblestones; wherever the children went, they brought their own small pile of pebbles with them.

'I can't stop now,' Sellass said when they ran up and touched her dress. 'I'm going to the lighthouse, then I have to deliver water.'

She waved goodbye, but the children followed her for a bit until one of them gave the signal, and they all turned and started running back towards the centre of town. Someone had seen the fat lady who often gave them something.

When Sellass eventually turned back towards Massawa, the centre of town was starting to wake up. Europeans strolled back and forth from the port to the Governor's Palace, hoping to find some cool air. No Eritrean girls were to be seen, only the ladies of the evening, and they sat in the bars and teccerie with their vermilion-painted lips, blooming like nocturnal flowers.

Sellass wished she could sit down on the ground and watch the evening unfold and listen to all the voices. It made her feel a part of the world; even if her role was small, she was one of the many actors who brought life to the streets in the centre of town.

She filled her waterskins and set off down the straight, dark road for Taulud. Sellass was afraid of figures passing in the shadows, the way they slipped by, their bare feet almost soundless on the cobblestones. To distract herself, she thought about her dream and Mariam's words. And while thinking about Mariam, she seemed to see the ghosts that people said walked across the waves at night under the starry sky, making their way to the pepper tree where Mariam sat waiting for them.

They came from the land of the dead, like an army of shades, to reveal the secrets of the living to the crippled woman who predicted the future.

When Sellass slept outdoors and heard the sound of the sea, she thought about those obscure presences and worried that she might actually see the spectres traversing the waves; in the moment that her fear grew most intense, she seemed to feel them breathing heavily on her, their exhalations weighing down on her body.

Even now, as she approached Taulud, she was afraid. She reassured herself by remembering that Mariam waited for those ghosts every single night, as if they were long-lost friends.

She entered the tukul and put down her waterskins. Her clothes and hair were drenched with sweat. The children and the elders of the large family sat on the floor eating their injera without speaking.

For a moment, in the feeble light, they looked like the shades of the dead that had been carried there by the sea.

5

When the Cristoforo Colombo dropped anchor in the harbour of Massawa, Carlo felt a crushing sense of despair, as if all the hope and joy he had experienced during the voyage were unsubstantiated lies that were fast dissolving in the steamy air.

It was early June, the beginning of the hottest season of the year in the small city, and it felt to Carlo, as he was disembarking, like they had arrived in hell. The heavy weight of the heat and humidity glued his clothes to his body. The blinding white light made him wish it were sundown already. Surely, there had to be night-time in this torrid nightmare of a country.

'Don't be scared,' Signorina Giuliana reassured him when they were on the pier. An elegant first-class passenger, the young lady had travelled there to visit her parents in Asmara, after concluding her studies in Italy. 'It becomes much more pleasant in October. Try and find a way of coming to the high plains; the climate in our area is wonderful.'

'If I make it to October,' Carlo said, watching her walk off in her light pink dress but lacking the strength to truly admire her physique. Gone were the nights when he fantasised about amorous encounters with the pretty passenger who had smiled at him once. Instead he sought out Maurizio, the young Venetian man he had befriended during the journey, to share his distress with him.

The passengers stood together on the pier, looking around in bewilderment, hoping to see someone who might reassure them of their futures, now that they were no longer safe in that large house on the sea.

The dock workers, both black and white, seemed entirely accustomed to the heat. They shouted among themselves in an incomprehensible language as they offloaded all sorts of merchandise, swearing and yelling in a mix of Tigrinya, Arabic and local dialects.

Carlo noticed a large man who looked to be the Ras of the harbour. He stood almost two metres tall, spoke with a southern Italian accent, and had a large tattoo of a woman's body across his broad chest: her long hair undulated with every breath the giant man took, and the words '*Amerò sempre Rosalia*' were written underneath.

Carlo later learnt that – despite the passionate declaration written across the man's chest expressing eternal love for some innocent woman waiting for his return in a remote mountain town of Calabria – Salvatore not only loved Rosalia but was also deeply passionate about all the sciarmutte in the town, and spent each night with a different one.

Il Duce sent young women from Italy to satisfy the needs and pleasures of the faraway sons of the fatherland, and especially so that the men would not touch the women of what was considered an inferior race. Salvatore never said no to a quick encounter with a generous white girl, but he always preferred the local women, Rosalia writhing across his chest with each heavy breath he took. The heat did not stop the tireless stevedore, day or night, and eventually there were many tiny Salvatores living on the streets of Massawa. Everyone knew the generous and fiery Calabrian, even the beggars who ran to bring him messages from various sciarmutte. To his credit, he always gave them a little change and knew all their names.

Carlo was given lodgings in the neighbourhood known as Gherar. He and Maurizio shared a room with a large ceiling fan, whose blades spun wildly in an effort to keep away both the heat and the mosquitoes. From their window they could see all the tonalities of the sea, which faded from the lightest green to the deepest blue. Carlo was assigned to railway construction, and his job, in the intense heat of Massawa, was exhausting. Sometimes, when the sun was high in the sky, his sight clouded over, the solar orb grew opaque, veiled by humidity, and splintered into countless other suns that fell through space, trailing blinding rays of light behind them, rolling one into the next, all the way down to the railroad tracks, where they exploded into a great fire that devoured the city and obliterated even the sea. With every passing day someone fell ill from heatstroke. Some of the men came back to work after a few days, others were never seen again. It was said that many young people died in the hospitals, especially Eritreans.

Despite the climate and the backbreaking work, after an initial period of confusion, Carlo got his bearings and soon fell in love with Massawa, discovering something new every day. He was fascinated by the diversity of the people in this small cosmopolis: the Jewish merchants, the Indian salesmen whose dusty shelves were piled high with bright fabrics, the

Arab tailors hunched over their sewing machines, the women vendors at the spice market, the Banyan protectors of the stray dogs – mangy but grateful creatures constantly hunting for both garbage and a master.

He admired the Indian women in their saris and the Muslim women with their veiled faces, but he had never seen girls as beautiful as the Eritreans, so proud and poised.

After sunset, the Italian ladies came out to stroll along the city streets, finally free of the bright sunlight that kept them sequestered inside their homes. Dressed in their pleated skirts and elegant hats, carrying fans and wearing Italian perfume, they walked arm in arm with their gentlemen, passing the time until cocktail hour.

One evening Carlo set out towards the lighthouse. He had heard that there was always a refreshing breeze in that spot.

He reached the boulders where the waves came galloping in like teams of horses, crashing and transforming into airy white foam and spray, the droplets shining in the last light of day.

Sitting on one of the boulders was a young Eritrean woman, not much older than a girl. She wore a crown of small braids on her head, the slow and careful work of Eritrean combers, heavy silver earrings that hung down to her shoulders, and a light and gauzy ankle-length dress.

The girl was startled by the sound of the arriving footsteps and turned to look at Carlo. He had never seen such a beautiful face. Her large, dark, slightly upturned eyes made him think of the stories from the *Thousand and One Nights* that Rita, his teacher, had read to him.

'Good evening,' Carlo said, coming to a halt. He realised that he had scared her and was worried she would run off, like one of the gazelles he sometimes saw on the dirt paths.

She did not reply but looked at him again, then scrambled down from the rocks. She covered her head and shoulders with a white futah and strode off.

'Stay,' Carlo said, gesturing for her not to leave. 'I won't bother you.'

But the girl walked off swiftly, staring straight ahead. Carlo could not help but follow her. He wanted to find out where she lived; he was suddenly worried that he would never see her again.

He followed her all the way to Gherar. When the girl went to pick up her waterskins, he gestured his willingness to help her, but she ignored him. It was as if she did not even see him.

When they reached the village of Taulud, it was already dark. At the entrance to her tukul, she turned around to look at him.

'What's your name?' Carlo asked, hoping that she would understand his words.

'Sellass,' the girl replied and went inside.

Carlo felt tired and confused. He did not want to walk all the way back to Gherar. Instead, he went and sat down at the foot of a tall palm tree not far from the sea. The tide was out and the air was pungently briny. He looked up at the immense and elaborate embroidery of distant lights and watched a few stars tumble down through space in a brief flash of brilliance, then disappear into nothingness.

Carlo thought about Sellass, Massawa, his village in Italy, and New York – a jumble of diverse thoughts and confused sensations.

And then, leaning against the trunk of the palm tree, he fell asleep.

In the dark of night, he saw gauzy futahs fly through the sky, all bearing the image of Sellass, her earrings rolling like waves.

A faraway drumming accompanied the dance of these veils. Soon that image faded and in its place Carlo saw his village. It was autumn: the trees, dropping copper and gold-coloured leaves, were laden with ripe fruit. He was sitting on a bus with silent, immobile elderly people. The bus travelled quickly along small village roads. Then the autumnal landscape and trees disappeared. He saw the red earth of Africa, the blue sky, that different light. The bus climbed up a steep hill to a covered market with a sign that said WATER & DEATH. Carlo got off the bus. The elderly people had all vanished. Under the roof of the market a number of fat black ladies dressed in bright clothes and clownish makeup busily tended to large pots of water. A long line of women, children, and elders wound all the way down the hill like a giant snake.

Devastated by poverty, people held out their bowls to be filled with water. There were swarms of flies everywhere, and the buzzing sound just kept growing louder. Then Sellass appeared. She had made her way up the hill on her own, carrying her pails. Carlo could hear her panting with effort from far away.

He woke up with a jolt. For a moment, he could not recall where he was.

Then he heard the sound of breathing nearby and he remembered his dream of Sellass. He got to his feet, deeply confused, as if he were on an unknown planet.

In the weak light that shone down from the stars, he saw a number of bodies lying nearby, both on the ground and on angarebs. Apparently people from the village had come there in search of cooler air.

Carlo snuck away, worried that someone might have seen him, and walked swiftly back to Gherar.

6

Carlo came down with a high fever for a few days after that. Fearing malaria, he was treated with quinine, but they said that it could have been anything; doctors had a hard time being precise in their diagnoses there.

Italian workers were frequently taken to the hospital for fevers from intestinal troubles or heatstroke. Some even died, at which point a letter would be sent to their relatives announcing the deaths of their loved ones in the name of the fatherland, which would forever be grateful for the men's ultimate sacrifice. Obviously, the letters were identical, all signed by some sweaty civil servant, sitting at his desk.

Carlo managed to avoid having one of those letters sent to his relatives. He was twenty-four years old, physically strong and he had never been gravely ill.

In a matter of days, the trembling and fever disappeared. Carlo drank litres of tea to replenish his body with fluids.

For the duration of his illness, on all those long nights that Carlo was forced to lay on a hot mattress, Maurizio had kept him company, showing him what a true friend he was by giving up his usual evening swim.

Maurizio kept his friend up to date on recent events: Tecle had been possessed by the demon Zar while at work, Raissa had slapped Salvatore and didn't want to see him ever again – but then she conceded him a long and tumultuous night of passion, the loud noises from which still echoed through the dark streets.

Following that night, which only increased Raissa's notoriety for being a 'sorceress of love,' and the slap, an officer had called for Salvatore and instructed him to stop chasing black sciarmutte, threatening him with jail time if he disobeyed. But someone had confided in Maurizio that the officer himself had a secret lover, a young Eritrean girl of great beauty, and that the man had wanted to hear all about Salvatore's night of passion, ostensibly to understand better what kind of evil spells this woman cast that caused such strong young men to fall prey to her.

As Carlo listened to the story about the Italian officer and the Eritrean girl with something akin to jealousy, he thought of the girl from the lighthouse. As soon as he was strong enough, he told Maurizio that he needed to go for a walk, and he made his way back there at sunset. Sellass was sitting exactly where he had seen her the first time. She looked at him, climbed down from the rock, threw her futah over her head and around her shoulders, and strode towards the centre of town.

'Maybe she's not the one sleeping with the officer,' Carlo told himself as he followed her, distancing the image of Sellass in the arms of the moustached man that Maurizio had described.

When they reached the path that led to Taulud, Carlo grabbed her arm and forced her to stop.

She did not fight him off. As a matter of fact, she had repeatedly returned to the lighthouse in the hopes of seeing him again, but feared that he would never come back.

She had watched the ships leaving the harbour and imagined that he had abandoned Massawa for his own village.

One day Tecle had come to the tukul in Taulud to inform Sellass that he had visited her relatives in Adi Ugri: they were well and sent their regards. Apparently her brother, Tesfai, had enrolled as an Ascaro soldier, to fight for the white man, and this had made his sisters very angry. Sellass, who had always disapproved of her brother's choice to first work and now fight for the white man in their own land, had suddenly felt ashamed of how she had been waiting for the boy with eyes the colour of the sea, the likes of which she had never seen before.

But she had put aside her uncertainty and had gone back to the lighthouse. Then, while staring out at the sea and thinking of him, she had heard his light footsteps on the pebbles. And now he was leading her down to the water in the dark and she was following him demurely, her heart beating fast, her head on fire.

Sellass became Carlo's woman. She learnt to pronounce his name and express herself in his language.

Carlo met with her in secret. He didn't want anyone else to know, except Maurizio. Soon, though, he realised that relationships with Eritrean women were tolerated – as long as they were not flaunted. Il Duce was far away; with that heat and those women no one could blame the young men for bending the laws to satisfy their personal tastes and desires.

When Sellass became pregnant, Carlo rented a small house near the salt flats from a Muslim merchant. Standing on its small terrace, they could see mountains of salt, blindingly bright in the sun, and still pools of rose-coloured water at their base.

7

Mariam looked up at the night sky: no stars, none of the shadowy figures who usually came to visit, only distant lightning. She gathered up her coins, tucked them into her bosom and crawled off, pulling herself along with her hands, dragging her crippled legs as if they were tree limbs struck by lightning. Slowly she made her way to her friend Zeudi's humble home, where she slept at night in exchange for a few coins.

As she was crawling past the mosque, a drunken sailor tripped over her. He yelled out, then fell to the ground and lay there, laughing and hiccupping. She was scared and could barely see him. All day she had felt a heaviness in her heart, together with the desire to disappear, to go to some faraway corner of the earth where she could die.

Sellass had come to visit her; she had brought some water and injera and wanted to know if the baby would be born with the new moon.

Mariam had been filled with dread even when Sellass was there, despite the girl's beauty and happiness. She hadn't wanted to toss her shells, it wasn't a good day to read the future. She knew that Sellass would soon have a little girl but the thought of the child scared Mariam, and she interpreted this fear as a presage of bad luck. She had not spoken to her old Muslim friend, Saleh, all day long. She had not seen the children who hid behind the pepper tree, trying to surprise her, either; with them she laughed and listened as they told her about the most recent ship to arrive, or about Mesfum, who had been forced to serve the colonel in silk pantaloons and a bright red cummerbund. The children often talked about Sellass: how she had become the woman of a white man who was always kind and generous with them; about their house on the salt flats and the silver anklets he had bought for her from Abramo; how she always stopped to talk and count pebbles with them on the street.

Nothing could banish the ominous feeling that Mariam sensed deep inside her that day. Now, paralysed by fear, pain coursing through her bones, as if the body that had tripped over her had been a boulder, she brought her sweaty palm to her chest to slow her pounding heart.

'Who are you?' the sailor asked in a gruff voice, crawling towards her.

Using all the strength she had, Mariam tried to back off, but the man pursued her, touching her shoulders, chest, belly and her poor legs.

'Are you pretty?' the sailor said, continuing to explore her body with his trembling hands.

Mariam took out some coins from her bosom and handed them to him. 'Here,' she said softly in Italian. 'Do you want my money?'

The sailor laughed and tossed her coins far away, then tore off the futah that Mariam wore around her shoulders. In her efforts to push him away, the man tumbled backwards onto the cobblestones, fell asleep and began to snore.

Mariam waited for her heart to stop beating so violently, then crawled over to the palm tree close to the mosque and leant against its trunk. She simply did not have the strength to continue on to Zeudí's house. She felt a storm approaching from a great distance.

It would not be long until the first rains of the season would finally allow the parched earth to exhale, breathing out a sense of wellbeing, practically a hymn of thanksgiving. Not long now until the much-desired music of rain would begin falling on rooftops and plants and on the happy faces of people looking upwards.

Mariam imagined herself back in Archico with her mother and brothers, peering into the sky as it darkened, casting a long shadow across the sea. She felt the first drops refresh her face and arms and soak her hair. Her mother used to thank God by pressing her forehead to the sand, her words melding with the sound of the falling rain.

As she recalled her childhood, Mariam allowed herself to tip slowly over and towards the ground. She had never felt this tired. Resting her ear on the ground, she thought she could hear breathing from unknown depths. She thought of the spirit of the earth, far below, in an unreachable place – the spirit that caused the heart of the earth to beat. And the sound of that breathing, which she managed to hear in the silence around her, brought her both peace and relief.

Then lightning illuminated the night sky and thunder made it quiver. The rain fell hard, sweeping away the great heat. Just like in Archico, Mariam could smell the scent of the damp earth.

She was found dead, just before dawn, by the muezzin who was on his way to prayer. Small and twisted, her dress and hair soaking wet, she looked like a tiny bird that had fallen from a branch. Word that Mariam the cripple had died spread quickly among the beggars of Massawa. Her young friends ran to the salt flats to inform Sellass, calling to her from a respectful distance.

A fat old woman stepped out onto the terrace and told them, rather rudely, to go away; Sellass had given birth during the night to a baby girl. Her name was Marianna.

8

Every day Sellass' friends came to the house on the salt flats to pick up Marianna and take her into the centre of town, to play pebbles with her on the shore, or to watch the ships come in. Sellass dressed the little girl in light white clothes, combed her copper curls, and watched her girlfriends take her off to play. She was expecting another child and hoped it would be a boy, that he would resemble Carlo.

When Carlo retreated, all alone, into his worlds of silence, Sellass was afraid he was thinking about leaving her, but then she immediately brushed away that fear. Carlo would always be there, and if he left, he'd take her with him to his country.

On the evenings that Carlo came from Gherar to be with them, Sellass did everything she could to make the house tidy and inviting. He brought them all sorts of gifts; the ships that arrived from Italy carried tinned goods, sweets, and other things that Sellass had never seen before. The days of famine she had experienced in Adi Ugri were long gone, and the man who had come from across the sea, the man whom Mariam had seen in the shells, took good care of her and Marianna. Sellass looked proudly at herself in a small mirror:

she had pretty clothes, silver ankle bracelets, a delicate gold ring and even a gold necklace.

If her sisters saw her now, they'd understand that she wasn't a white man's servant, but his woman. When Sellass thought about how surprised people in the village would be to see what a lady she'd become, she smiled to herself. One day she'd go back to Adi Ugri, bring them gifts and introduce them to her children.

Occasionally Maurizio came to see them at the house. One evening he brought Marianna a white baby goat with a bell around its neck, and the child laughed when she heard the bleating animal.

Carlo adored Marianna, he taught her to speak and walk, and he stayed with her at night until she fell asleep. Looking down on her as she slept, he couldn't imagine her and Sellass in his country, with its cold winters; it was as if they were creatures of the sun and their glow would fade in other lands. At the same time, he couldn't imagine himself living his entire life in Africa, in that house on the salt flats. When thoughts like that troubled him, he became melancholic and taciturn, even as Sellass continued to sing around the house.

When little Gianfranco was born, Sellass had never felt happier – the child had dark skin and green eyes. Everyone admired the baby, Maurizio said he had never seen such a beautiful child.

When Gianfranco grew older and Sellass carried him in her arms down the streets of Massawa, even the European ladies stopped to admire the child, with his blond hair and light green eyes.

Everyone knew that Carlo had fathered two children with an Eritrean girl, but he often spent the night in the

Gherar lodgings because he feared the consequences of having two mixed-race children. People said it wasn't good for an Italian man to live with one of the locals; eventually he'd get stuck, they said, trapped in the sand. Il Duce's laws clearly forbade Italian men from sleeping with women of an inferior race, and men who had children with them could be arrested and imprisoned for anywhere from one to five years. There were rumours that Maurizio had a lover too, a beautiful Greek woman: the bored wife of a wealthy Greek merchant who often travelled for business. Better to sleep with another man's wife than with a local girl and have bastard children, they said. Lots of men, even older ones, had lost their heads for local girls, but eventually they either returned home to their wives and left their offspring to fate, or never even learnt that they had fathered children.

One morning Carlo was summoned by Major Donati, a decent fellow, known and liked in Massawa, a man as fond of cigars as he was of bridge.

'Cinzi,' the major began in a fatherly tone, 'we all know you've had two beautiful children with a local black girl. Officially, I don't know a thing, or else, my dear Cinzi, you'd be in prison. The law is clear on the matter and, as of last year, there's no ignoring it. Now, I don't want to ruin your life, but you need to know that I'm running a risk here, and I can't just keep turning a blind eye on the situation. And please don't tell me, my dear friend, that you're in love with the pretty little savage.'

Carlo was speechless. What problems was his little family creating? What kind of risk did they present? He took good care of them after all.

Major Donati went on: 'Would you like me to make arrangements for you to return to Italy? You could leave her some money. These people don't need much to get by and they forget easily. They don't have feelings like we do. They're different, believe me.'

Carlo looked at the man, he was being earnest with him. Carlo felt deeply unhappy.

'For the moment, I'd rather not return to Italy,' Carlo said. 'One day, maybe. And actually, sir, I don't agree that these people don't have feelings. All that's different about them is the colour of their skin.'

'You're young, you don't have experience in these matters,' the man replied patiently. 'You'll understand in due course. I'm tired of hearing stories like this and have no intention of ruining my career over it. Last night I had to arrest Salvatore for beating up a young man who had recently arrived from Italy. They were in a tecceria that belonged to one of those sciarmutte and the new fellow had already got a whiff of the local women. We had to shut the tecceria down: there was simply too much talk going on about one particular woman, rumours that risked compromising decent people. Can you believe it? They say that she even prepares magic potions to make our men lose their heads. Salvatore was constantly there, he follows her everywhere. A little prison time will be good for him, cool him down. No sense ruining your life for a couple of nights with an African sciarmutta. For goodness' sake, Il Duce sent us some splendid women from our own country, pretty and affectionate girls, too good, really, for just a couple hours of pleasure. Cinzi, you've taken care of the girl, she knows how lucky she is, but you have nothing to gain from such a union. You know how we try to help you men, meeting you halfway. We know how difficult it is to live here, how hard the work is. But we simply can't let laws be broken so openly, in broad daylight, so to speak. What would happen if everyone took up with black girls and had bastard children? Don't put me in a difficult spot, Cinzi. Let me repeat: I ought to have already arrested and booked you. I can't have one rule for you and another for everyone else.'

The major fidgeted nervously with some documents on his desk, then looked at the large portrait of Il Duce hanging on the wall. 'For now, I know nothing,' he said with a sigh. 'But you must return to your house in Gherar each night and never be seen with that girl and the children in public. And if anyone asks, you say they're not yours. Do you understand me? Otherwise I will be forced to take action.'

He then lowered his voice and offered Carlo a mint. 'They say your woman is young and beautiful. But you'll see, in a few years, she'll be ready for the scrapheap. You know how they are: at twenty, they're already old and withered.' The major stood up and held out his hand to conclude the matter. 'I won't have you sent back because you're a hard worker,' he said. 'But listen to me. Follow my advice – fine, let's call them "orders." One day you'll have a beautiful Italian wife and you'll forget all about this little adventure.'

Carlo left the office filled with apprehension. But gradually, as he walked, a vague sense of calm and wellbeing returned to him. He thought of the children and of Sellass, he imagined her on the terrace of their house on the salt flats, waiting for evening, poised and proud, ready to silently fulfil his every desire, welcoming all his moods. And yet he knew he couldn't stay with them forever.

9

One evening, around sunset, the flamingos arrived. They came gliding in on the small pools of water at the foot of the salt mountains, one by one, then stood there on their skinny legs without moving, their long necks twisted as if they were studying their reflections in the water. When the birds flew off again, forming an immense pattern of pinkish feathers that sparkled in the evening sunlight, Marianna started to cry, begging her mother to make them come back. Sellass tried to soothe her and told her about a special place on the coast, a little strip of land all covered with plants, where the birds went to sleep at night and where all the stars that fell out of the sky were reunited. Once Mariam had told Sellass about such a place: she had said that the shades brought all the stars they found there, that each time there was a falling star – their skies were crowded with stars – one of the shades from the distant kingdom of the dead would pick it up and bring it back to that strip of land along the coast.

Marianna did not understand all the stories that Sellass told her but she sat quietly and listened to her, touching her mother's face now and then with her little hand as if to make sure that she was real.

Later Marianna tried to tell Carlo the story about the birds with the big pink wings but when she remembered that they had flown away she started to cry again.

The following day Carlo built a kite. He worked on it for a long time, using paper, bamboo and a paste made from flour and water.

Gianfranco, who was now two years old and never sat still, was enchanted by the way his father made this mysterious toy come to life. Marianna could not wait to see the paper bird take to the skies.

Maurizio was there that day, too. The children loved Maurizio because he always brought them something, and he played and laughed with them. Sellass helped out by asking if they needed more flour or water to complete the project. Then they went – all together, even Sinai, the little girl who came from Taulud to help Sellass – to a nearby field. There was a light breeze, Carlo tossed the kite into the air and let out some string.

Uncertainly at first, and then ever more confidently, the kite started to climb up into the sky. The fringe on its tail quivered with every gust of wind. Sinai clapped her hands with joy and Sellass laughed, one hand over her eyes to protect them from the blinding light. The kite hesitated for a moment, as if on a wave, and then climbed higher; Marianna held on tightly to Carlo, she was scared that the paper bird would fly off to the small piece of land that her mother had told her about. Suddenly, other children appeared as if out of nowhere, as if summoned by magic, laughing and whooping to see the kite in the sky. Gianfranco tried to run with them and mimicked their gestures.

They flew the kite for three days before it got stuck in the single tall and sickly-looking palm tree that grew on the salt flats, and since the kite was by then a little tattered – from tiny grabbing hands – they left it there. No one cried. The children looked at the flying contraption for a few minutes and then waved goodbye to it. A crow sitting in the palm tree cawed.

Carlo had no time to build another kite. There was talk of imminent war, people had been discussing the threat for some time, a sense of alarm and tension filled the air; Italy could potentially be drawn into the conflict between the great European nations. Many people claimed that Mussolini would never go to war but this certainty grew weaker with every passing day.

10

Carlo sat at a café in the centre of town with some of his fellow workers. They were discussing the conflict in Europe and Italy's probable entry into the war.

An Arab fisherman came in – short, elderly, so emaciated his bones jutted out at all angles, his face worn down by the sun and age – and made his way over to Carlo. He rested his heavy straw *zembil* on the ground, it was laden with starfish and seashells, and smelt of the sea. He then took a pouch out of his pocket and opened it: pearls of different sizes shone like moonlight in his dark palm.

'I have pearls,' the old man said.

'Enough of these pearls,' Maurizio said, waving him away. 'As soon as we sit down, you arrive with your pearls and other creatures.'

The old man was not deterred. Maurizio, seeing that Carlo was interested in haggling, intervened on his behalf. They spread out the pearls on the table to better examine them. The old man, after lengthily praising the splendour and shape of each one of the jewels of the sea, eventually and unwillingly, as if it were demeaning for him to do so, gave them the prices, which of course, he noted, was virtually impossible given how beautiful the pearls were. For a brief moment, staring at those tiny objects of vast beauty, all talk of war was forgotten.

'I don't think Eritrean women like pearls,' Maurizio said, weighing out two gems in his hand. 'They prefer gold and silver.'

Carlo did not say a word. He chose two and tucked them safely in his pocket. He was in a bad mood, afraid that the war would disrupt their little world. Several important battles had already taken place in Abyssinia; Italian soldiers were fighting the Abyssinians who struggled to defend their country. A number of military commanders had come to Massawa over the years, sent there by Il Duce to subjugate the rebels. Abyssinia was being forced to bow down and become part of the growing empire. And whenever any steely generals came ashore from their battlecruisers, there was much fanfare and enthusiasm.

A reception was always held in the Governor's Palace, where the lights shone brightly to welcome their friends and the ladies dressed up like Cinderella for a ball. Such grand occasions, filled with warm smiles and euphoric proclamations, were a way for the Italians to honour their distant homeland. Eritrean waiters in light-coloured pantaloons and red cummerbunds rushed through the grand halls, as the governor demanded the utmost efficiency and precision for the great lords of war. But the Abyssinian campaign and its generals faded in importance when news started arriving from Italy about the conflict between the superpowers. Everyone tried to predict what the future would bring. Maurizio claimed that Mussolini would not let himself get involved, while others said that Italy would soon go to war. Still others claimed that there would definitely be war, but that it would be brief.

Carlo often spent the night in Gherar, discussing the matter with Maurizio, allowing his fears to be allayed by his friend's calm and reassuring tone. But in the middle of the night, when he could not sleep and the hours seemed to stand still, he thought about imminent disaster. At times like that, the sounds of the night – the howling of a jackal, the call of a solitary owl – were sinister omens. Carlo had to get up and out of bed and seek peace down by the water; he would listen to the sound of the waves splashing against a passing fishing boat and look up at the stars. He could almost feel them vibrating in the darkness.

The news of war came on a day of intense heat, the hot season had already begun. Carlo was at work on the railway when a colleague came running over. It was Mario, a young man, new to Massawa, who had been nicknamed 'the writer' for how he spent his evenings writing to his mother and the kind-hearted girls back in Italy who offered to correspond with the soldiers in East Africa.

'It's war!' Mario yelled. 'We're at war! Mussolini has sided with the Germans. Everyone's meeting at the Savoia at six o'clock tonight.'

There was general mayhem, and even the Eritrean labourers felt involved in the upheaval. Carlo finished his shift and then went to Gherar to wash up. He dressed carefully, as if for an important meeting, took the pearls out of his drawer, wrapped some bills in a piece of newspaper, and told Maurizio that he would see him the following day, he would not be joining them at the Savoia. He then set off towards the salt flats with a heavy heart, wishing he could disappear, that he had never heard of Massawa, Sellass, or the children. He looked out at the island of Sheik Said; it had not changed, it was still there, with its mangroves and flocks of seabirds. Nature remained calm, indifferent to the great events that affected mankind. The mangroves would continue to grow on the island, every evening the seabirds would flock back to their nests in the tangled shrubs at the water's edge.

When Carlo reached the house, he told Sellass to leave the children with Sinai and join him in the bedroom, that he needed to talk to her. Sellass did not seem upset but she never showed her emotions, not through her facial expressions or her voice. Carlo looked at the cross tattooed on her wide forehead and at her large dark eyes, in which he saw something of Marianna's gaze. It was in that moment, right when he urgently needed to talk to Sellass, that he realised that what had always disturbed him about his daughter's face was the profound sadness, the remoteness, in her eyes.

'Sellass,' he said, forcing himself to focus on the moment at hand, which he so wished he could avoid. 'You have to leave here. You have to take the children and leave, go back to your village. We're at war and you're in danger here. In Adi Ugri you will be safe.'

Sellass did not reply. She sat very still. Even her breathing was quiet.

'Do you understand me, Sellass?' Carlo asked. 'You have to take the children away immediately. You can take the bus, tomorrow I will find someone to travel with you.'

Sellass continued to look at him without speaking.

'I brought you some money,' Carlo added. 'So that you can take care of the children.'

Sellass looked down at the floor. Carlo realised what she wanted to ask him.

'For now, I'll stay here,' he said. 'And we will be reunited in better times. Don't be scared, it won't last long.'

In the shadows of the room, it seemed to him that she was still a child. She no longer wore braids like she did when they first met, she now straightened her hair, but she still wore the same long dress and futah. She painted her hands and feet with henna and always walked barefoot; he had never managed to convince her to wear sandals.

'You,' Sellass finally found the courage to say in her faltering Italian. 'You will stay here?'

'I told you,' Carlo said. 'I will stay, but you and the children must leave. We will be together again soon.'

Sellass went and opened a drawer, took out some objects and articles of clothing, and laid them out carefully on the bed. The expression on her face did not change. Carlo watched as she placed her things in a sack, as if she had to leave in a matter of minutes. He wanted to give her the pearls but did not dare. She seemed to be ignoring him.

That night, while everyone was sleeping, Sellass left the house and walked down to the water. She needed some fresh air and could not breathe; she spread out her futah on the terrace and waited for sleep to come to her, but in vain.

She sat on the boulders, the waves gently splashing up against her legs, the golden quarter moon illuminating a strip of sea. There, in that glow, Sellass saw Mariam: she was crawling across the surface of the water, dragging her poor, twisted legs behind, her faded futah wrapped over her head and shoulders. Behind Mariam came a procession of shades, each one carrying a star. Sellass trembled, she felt cold, sweat ran down her back and between her breasts. She squeezed her eyes shut; she did not want to see Mariam or the procession of shades, she was scared they would take her away to that distant kingdom where time ended all human breath, forever. Even though a few moments earlier she had wanted to die, now she was scared. Now she wanted to run back to the safety of their small home.

With great effort and holding her breath, she managed to stand up and open her eyes. She looked out at the sea. A boat glided across the strip of light on the water. Then the boat disappeared, swallowed up by the darkness. Mariam was not there, nor was the procession of shades. The stars continued to shine in the sky.

Sellass remembered the day that Mariam told her that she would meet a man from across the sea, but the time was not right, the crippled woman had said, to get clear answers from the shells; the image had been clouded with fog.

Sellass returned to the house, to the angareb on the terrace, but sleep still evaded her. Soon after, she heard Carlo's light footsteps. She saw him bend down over her.

'Sellass, Sellass,' Carlo whispered to her, loosening her hair, removing her long white dress, slipping off her bracelets.

'Sellass, Sellass,' he said, her name echoing through the moonlit sky.

Then Sellass felt a sharp pain in her chest as she recalled that those moments would soon end. If only Mariam had been there to see the future, to say a single word, one word was all she needed; but now Mariam was one of the shades that travelled across the sea at night.

Carlo kissed her smooth skin, damp with sweat and sea spray and, as if in a dream, she felt herself dissolve into a foamy wave. As the wave broke across the terrace, Carlo felt the salt water on his face and hands; then it returned towards its creator, the sea, with a gentle lapping noise.

Carlo waited for time to pass, for the moon and tide to change, for the wave to leave the sea and return to him.

Time went by, generations came and went, but the wave did not return. Soon the terrace was overgrown with grass, bushes, shrubs, mangroves and palm trees. Pelicans and flamingos arrived to make their nests there, terns called loudly, chasing people away from the terrace. The kite that hung in the palm tree grew immense, offering shade in the hours when the sun was at its hottest. Multicolour orchids grew between slender bamboo canes, and often, in order not to feel lonely, the kite sometimes talked about its long journey towards the heavens.

Carlo sat there without moving, just waiting, for years. But the wave did not return. His hair grew long and shone like gold in the sun, the perfect place for small transparent birds to build their nests. His eyes disintegrated from staring out to sea for so many years, and the hollowed orbs became a resting place for fireflies, those wandering lanterns of the night.

When Carlo awoke, the sky looked like a large piece of faded slate, with dawn erasing all trace of stars, decorating it with streamers of gold, red and blue, preparing a celebration for the sun, which would soon rise out of the sea.

Carlo observed Sellass, then gently caressed her face to wake her. He could not hear her breathing, her luminous skin had gone cold, her eyelashes did not move. It was as if she had fallen asleep forever.

11

Sellass and her children set out on their long journey, travelling by bus and mule. The children were excited by the novelty and did not complain at all. Marianna tended carefully to Gianfranco, giving him water to drink even when he didn't want any, reassuring him that the mule was their friend, that they could trust him, that he would carry them to their mother's village in the high plains where there was no sea but the air was cool.

They reached Adi Ugri one evening around sunset. When they got close to the tukul that used to belong to her parents, Sellass had the children descend from the mule and they made their way to the house on foot. Sitting outside, on the ground, were her five sisters and Meret, her sister-in-law. They were praying and had all shaved their heads. Sellass knew instantly that a relative had died; she thought immediately of Tesfai, her brother.

When the women saw her approach, they got to their feet and looked at the children she held by the hand. They did not walk towards her or kiss or embrace her, as they ought to have done, according to custom.

Sellass stood still and looked at their shorn heads, the sign of mourning filling her with sorrow.

'Tesfai is dead,' Mebrat said, without showing any emotion at her sister's return. 'He was killed while fighting for the Italians. He died for them, those awful people who have tried to take our country from us, with all their stealing and killing.' She looked at the children. 'Who are these children?' she asked. 'Are they yours?'

Sellass nodded.

'So you, too, sided with the white man. And now you have bastard children…'

Marianna squeezed her mother's hand tightly; she did not know the meaning of the word that Mebrat had used, but she'd certainly never forget it, and realised that it was as much of an offence to them as it was for Sellass. She glared at Mebrat.

'I did not serve the white people,' Sellass said. 'My children's father is a good Italian man who takes care of us. I live in a beautiful home. He is very generous and he loves our people.'

'So why are you here?'

'There is war. It is not safe in Massawa now, not with the children. I would like to stay here for a while, in the village. I have money and can take care of everyone.'

'We don't want money from the people who killed our brother. You'll never see that man again, Sellass. You're just a poor innocent girl that a white man used for a time. With the excuse of war, he sent you and the children back here so that he can return to his country and marry a white woman.'

A heavy sense of oppression came over Sellass. She wished she could cry, throw herself down on the ground, show the pain she felt inside.

'I will be reunited with him when the war is over,' she said calmly. 'He is a good man and he loves the children. He will not return to his country.'

Marianna squeezed her mother's hand even tighter and Gianfranco started to cry; he was sleepy, exhausted from the journey. Meret came up to them, smiled at Marianna and ran her hands through the little boy's blond hair, marvelling at the colour of his eyes.

'Do not speak that way in front of the children,' Meret said, looking back at Mebrat and walking over to embrace Sellass.

'You can't stay here,' Mebrat said, looking at both Sellass and Meret to show her disapproval. 'We have enough troubles of our own. We don't need these bastard children, they're not members of our family.'

Meret picked up Gianfranco. 'Come, Sellass,' she said. 'You can stay with me.'

As they were talking, a number of children came out of nearby tukuls and alleyways. They were wearing rags; clusters of flies swarmed around their faces and their large beautiful eyes.

The children looked in amazement at Marianna and Gianfranco and then started giggling and whispering among themselves. Tesfai and Meret's children were among them; they rushed over to their mother, who held the child with the golden hair in her arms, and grabbed her dress tightly to show that she belonged to them.

Marianna looked suspiciously at the children.

'They're making fun of us,' she said to her mother. 'Let's leave.'

'They just don't know you,' Meret said, trying to reassure Marianna while rocking Gianfranco in her arms as he continued to cry. 'They've never seen children with hair like yours. But you'll make friends with them soon enough.'

'My father says I have copper-colour hair,' Marianna said, relaxing a little and running her hands through her wavy locks, as if to show the young onlookers just how pretty her hair was.

Mebrat and her sisters returned to their tukul, scolding the children who continued to huddle around Sellass and shooing them away.

'I can go and stay with Alefesc,' Sellass said to Meret, unfastening her bags from the mule. 'She won't turn me away.'

'Alefesc is no longer with us. She was constantly tormented by the Zar; we took her to the priest countless times, Ghebre stayed with her for months and gave her the strongest herbal potions that exist, but the demon never left her. She howled and yelled during the day and, at night, she wandered through the valley and into the mountains. One day she vanished. We looked for her for a long time, everyone helped, but we never found her, dead or alive. The hyenas must've eaten her.'

Sellass recalled listening to her aunt's magical stories and was certain that Alefesc would have loved her children. Her thoughts also went to Tesfai, how they used to spend all their time together, running through nearby valleys, trying not to think about their constant hunger, looking for things to eat in the bushes, among the rocks, hoping that someone would bring a handful of flour to them in the tukul before nightfall so they could make some *borgutta* or injera.

She remembered how her parents had worked those clods of earth for their whole lives – which was not that long, really – and how, in the one year of abundance they had known, when there was food on the table each and every day, her father had been forced to count out the few coins he had and pay taxes to the Ras, giving him almost everything he had.

Before going to sleep, Sellass prayed long and hard that her brother Tesfai had reached the distant land of shades. Then she looked at the two pearls that Carlo had given her on her final morning on the terrace that she loved so much. They were like two drops of moonlight with hints of pale blue; tears maybe, Sellass thought, that fell from the moon into the sea on the nights it felt most alone.

That night Sellass slept on the ground, next to her children. She told them that it was customary in those parts to sleep on nothing but a futah, and they did not complain. Marianna lay close by, resting a tiny hand on her mother's face.

12

'Why did you send them away?' Maurizio asked, clearly displeased with his friend.

'Because war will come here, too,' Carlo said. 'At least in her village they'll be safe.'

'I don't think there will be fighting in Massawa. They could've stayed.'

Carlo sat down on the side of the bed. 'I want to leave,' he said, staring out of the open window at the sea. 'I want to get away before I'm forced to fight.'

'And how will you manage that?' Maurizio asked in shock.

'On a container ship going to some other country in Africa, or Asia. If you're willing to pay, they'll find room for you.'

'You'd be a deserter. And if they catch you, that'll be the end of you. We're at war now, we're already soldiers.'

'I'm not staying,' Carlo repeated. 'I have to find a way.'

'What about Sellass? And the children? What about them? Or are you just like all the others, ready to leave your women and children behind?'

'I've taken care of everything. I've given her some money. One day the war will be over and then I'll come back. I'm not going to stick around and get killed for that girl, I'm sick of hearing people talk about war.'

Maurizio made his way to the door, visibly upset. 'That girl, as you call her,' he said before leaving, 'is your woman, and she loves you more than you can imagine, but maybe you just can't see that. She would never leave you, not even if she were in extreme danger. She's not even twenty years old and has to bring up two children all alone. I wish you hadn't sent her away, I can only imagine her fear, the anguish of returning to her village, after so many people left it. And your children: now they'll have to get used to living like all the other little black kids in the village, after growing up in a comfortable, modern home. I just can't believe you did that,' he said and walked out, slamming the door behind him.

Carlo stood there, staring at the sea. It was one of those sunsets that cast a golden glow through the sky and across the sea, making the horizon line melt into liquid gold, causing all other hues to disappear: the blues and greens of the sea, the deep azure sky, they were nothing but a single blaze of gold. The entire scene looked like it had been created by a story-teller, someone capable of imagining golden lakes in the heavenly clouds for fairies and sprites to bathe in before taking part in their magical night-time ceremonies.

Carlo was enchanted by the scene in front of him. He focused on it as if trying to memorise it with both his heart and his mind, so that he would never forget it, or the profound emotions it aroused in him. Then the gold faded into the muted shadows of night, bringing Carlo some relief. It was too much for one man's small heart to sustain so much intense and mysterious beauty.

He sat down at his desk and opened his old atlas. He studied the drawings of Africa, gently tracing his finger around the different seas and islands, across mountain chains and lands covered with snow and immense forests.

'I could go to South Africa,' he thought to himself. 'It's a common destination for merchant ships.'

He walked out and headed towards the harbour. Salvatore the Calabrian sat on the pier smoking a cigarette. Rosalia lay resting on this chest, moving ever so slightly with his breathing. Her long mermaid hair covered her breasts and belly, so that Salvatore would not flare up with jealousy when people ogled her.

'Salvatore,' Carlo asked him. 'Are any merchant ships going to South Africa?'

Salvatore smiled at him complicitly.

'You want to cut the cord? If I had your girl, I'd live on a volcano for her.'

Salvatore spoke in a blend of Italian and Calabrian, adding a word in Tigrinya now and then to show that he knew the language.

'I'm asking for a friend,' Carlo replied curtly. 'Besides, it seems to me that you have no lack of girls to choose from,' he added. For some time, Salvatore had been living with a thirteen-year-old girl from Dankalia, paying off her family with a large part of the money he had saved up for his marriage to the patient Rosalia.

'A beauty,' Salvatore sighed, slapping his hairy thigh with his broad hand. 'So beautiful it drives you crazy – and good, too. Obedient, day and night. You know how they are.'

Carlo looked at the unwitting Rosalia and the banner of words under her feet.

'A man can't survive here, far from home, in this deathly heat, with this work, without a woman. A man is a man; he needs a woman. For them, it's different.' Salvatore sighed, inadvertently caressing his Rosalia. 'And now there's this fucking war. Who knows where we'll end up. Let's just hope the fighting doesn't come here.'

'Salvatore, do me a favour: you're the boss around here, after all.' Carlo knew that the Calabrian liked to feel important. 'Find out if there's a merchant ship bound for South Africa and let me know. I'd be deeply grateful. I'll come back and see you tomorrow.'

'I know that a small ship is leaving in a few days for those parts, South Africa or somewhere around there. I'll talk to Antonio, I'll find out for you,' he said with a wink.

Salvatore always went to great lengths to help his friends, he was a generous man at heart. He put Carlo in touch with someone who could help him board a ship as a stowaway in exchange for a little cash. All the arrangements had been made but then the ship's departure was delayed.

It left the port fifteen days later than the original sail date, after Carlo's contact was arrested for illegal trafficking. As a result, Carlo's escape plan failed; the ship could not risk taking on any stowaways at that time.

The war eventually reached Africa: Italian soldiers fought against the English on Eritrean soil. Carlo was terrified at the prospect of going into battle and thought only about his escape.

It did not take long for Italy to lose its hold on the colonies. Soon enough, the English were victorious in Eritrea.

Months of great chaos and fear passed, with many Italians returning home definitively. The atmosphere changed, even in Massawa. Gone were the days of great hopes, when the collective goal was to build an empire, when people sang songs like 'Faccetta nera.'

The port was off-limits. Carlo no longer knew whom to turn to, everything became so difficult. Salvatore left. Raissa, who managed to reopen her tecceria thanks to the protection of an influential Greek friend, knew everything and told everyone Salvatore's story. The Calabrian had gone to Dankalia and joined a group of nomadic shepherds; he left Massawa at night, guided by his young woman. He had often spoken of that colourful volcanic region. He never returned to Massawa and never went back to the Calabrian mountains, where Rosalia surely continued to wait for him, preferring to wear black for the rest of her life and think he had died a hero's death rather than imagine him happy among the splendid local women. If anyone had ended up getting 'trapped in the sand,' it was Salvatore, who continued to wander through the dunes with more than one Rashaida woman by his side.

Carlo felt calm. He went to see the house on the salt flats, it had been closed up, no one had lived there since the day they left it. Apparently the owner had left for Mecca but never returned. They said he had been thrown overboard by the owner of the dhow he was travelling on, and that it was all because of money.

Carlo made his way back to the field where he had flown the kite; he could still see Sellass, her hand shielding her eyes from the sunlight, the children excited and happy about their new toy. In his memory, the images of the past were tinged with the melancholy light of dreams as they begin to fade, when the dawn starts to erase the joyful visions of night. And the beauty he saw on those small faces, the memory of which he conserved deep inside, untouched by time, filled him with profound despair.

When Carlo eventually turned back towards Gherar, it was with the thought that he would never again return to the salt flats. He wanted to forget their times together entirely.

An English officer was waiting for him outside his house, together with a soldier who stood at attention, staring out at the horizon as if searching for a sign.

Maurizio was gone, Carlo never heard from him again. The officer gestured for Carlo to follow him: he was under arrest.

Nothing was explained to him at the barracks. They merely read his personal details off a piece of paper and told him that he had to wait, just like everyone else, to find out which prison camp he would be sent to, in which country.

Many men were arrested in those days and sent to prison camps. The laws of war were implacable: there were the victors and the vanquished. And all it took was for someone, even a neighbour acting out of spite, to mention a name, and a man's life could be ruined.

13

Sellass remained in Adi Ugri only a few days. She knew almost straight away that they could not stay there. Her sisters never spoke to her. Not even Mesfin, with whom she had spent so much time as a child, dared speak to her, fearing the divine punishment invoked by Mebrat for all who disobeyed her orders.

Meret was kind and affectionate and told Sellass that Tesfai would have been glad to host her, but Sellass felt ill at ease there. There were so many of them in one room, the children were always crying for one reason or another. Essentially nothing had changed, the village was still home to misery and poverty.

It occurred to Sellass that she needed to find a way of making money, so as not to spend what Carlo had given her. If her man never returned – a thought that sickened her, but which she couldn't get out of her head – she'd need a house. If she saved carefully, she might be able to buy one, but it would have to be in a city. She definitely needed to leave the village.

She considered Asmara, where she had spent six or seven days when Marianna had been scalded by boiling hot coffee.

Carlo had sent Sellass and the child there because of the properly equipped hospital and expert doctors, fearing that Marianna would remain disfigured. The child was well cared for, her burns were not serious, and overall Sellass had had a positive impression of the city, with all its people, shops, markets and paved roads. But when she returned to Massawa, to her man and the sea, she promptly forgot about that city in the mountains.

As she mulled over her uncertain future, she realised Asmara was her only choice.

And so one day she left, but not before carefully explaining to Meret that if someone came looking for her, sent there by Carlo, she should relay a message to her in Asmara; Sellass would reimburse her for the trouble, they would be able to find her through the Coptic church, she would leave her address with the priest.

Sellass and her children moved to Edaga Arbi, a neighbourhood on the outskirts of the city comprised of huts made of mud and straw, and shacks made of cement and tin. The earth was red and billowed up around them in clouds with each gust of wind. A few prickly pear plants gave the area a hint of green, while cattle and goats grazed on patches of faded grass in an effort to alleviate their hunger.

Now and then donkeys with large rheumy eyes, laden with brimming waterskins, passed by, driven by children in rags who beat them with gnarled sticks, trying to get them to trot. Groups of children sat in the sun for hours on end, staring into nothingness. Those with a little energy, the ones who somehow managed to eat every day, kicked up their heels and ran around yelling and inventing all sorts of games with whatever they found: some wire, a rock, shreds of paper.

At the first light of dawn, a procession of beggars set out towards the centre of Asmara where they spent their days asking for alms, trying to move people to pity through their misfortunes, hoping to bring back a little change, enough to pay for a scant meal.

Among them were the blind, who made their way forward by holding on to the shoulders of children, who guided them until they spied a potential benefactor. At that point, the blind folk, although accustomed to moving through darkness, would waver unsteadily and fall but they always managed to get to their feet somehow. Then came the cripples, who trailed their deformed limbs behind them; over time they had learnt how to move with relative ease, some of them relying on tin cans to protect their hands as they pulled themselves across the rocky terrain. Then there were the lepers: an ageless woman, part of her face eaten away by the illness, which got worse with each passing day, and a man who sat outside a bakery, from which came the aroma of freshly baked bread, with a rag over his deformed face. Every so often someone dropped a coin at his feet. The procession of beggars returned to Edaga Arbi after sundown, seeming hardly human in the evening shadows, seeking relief in the oblivion of night.

Friday was market day. Men, women and children climbed the hill to the neighbourhood and eagerly set up shop, swiftly setting out their goods on mats on the ground: piles of charcoal, incense, teff, Berbere, *shiro*, kohl powder, henna, empty tins. The air was woven thick with voices, hymns were sung to dura and onions, every item had endless qualities to be praised. Hens and roosters, their talons tied, hopped about as if possessed by demons, crying out even louder than the merchants themselves.

A few goats, resigned to their destiny, bleated dejectedly. On market days everyone came out of their dwellings to look at the goods for sale or to bargain loudly. In the evening, after everyone returned inside, the scent of spices and incense hung in the air.

Sellass had to settle for the poor dwelling she had managed to rent for little money, believing it to be a temporary solution. The house was essentially one large room, its only furnishings consisted of a wobbly table and two angarebs, and there were holes in the roof.

The house had a courtyard surrounded by a crumbling wall, the top of which was embedded with shards of glass to discourage potential thieves from breaking into the squalid home. Around there, even a piece of wood was considered precious and could be used for something. In one corner of the courtyard stood a beautiful bright green bush that attracted loudly chirping birds. The plant seemed so proud of its flourishing foliage – all its little branches were covered with tiny leaves – that it almost appeared conscious of its wasted beauty; it was born by mistake, from a seed carried there by the wind from some faraway garden.

Marianna and Gianfranco looked around their new home with astonishment. All these changes were sources of continual surprise, the important thing was that their mother was nearby. They never asked about their father; Sellass had told them he'd join them one day but for this to happen they should never talk about him.

Sellass started looking for a job but refused to work for white people.

'You have no choice,' an old Coptic priest told her once. She had left her address with him as soon as she settled in

Edaga Arbi. 'Italians are good people, you had two children with one of them. You sinned, Sellass, and now you have to think of your children. Go in peace and serve the white people.'

But Sellass did not want to work for an Italian family. As a result, over time, she was forced to spend some of the money that she had been trying to save. Even though she bought little and their meals were humble, the money for their future house started to dwindle.

She sold her silver anklets to a merchant in the centre of town to replace the coins she had taken out of the pouch that she kept hidden away.

One evening, someone knocked on their door. Marianna ran to open it with great excitement, thinking it was her father who had come to take them away from there and back to the house by the sea.

Instead it was Ahmed, the Muslim man who, so many years before, had asked Sellass to become his bride. Even when he was with other women, Ahmed dreamt of Sellass: he imagined her slender body in her light dress, how she walked down the street, even when she was a child. He had never stopped watching her, even after she became Carlo's woman – so beautiful and proud – and he had always hoped that one day something would happen that would allow him to finally make her his own.

It was a tense encounter. When Sellass saw him, she was reminded of happy times in Massawa, back when she used to carry water and stop to talk to her crippled friend, Mariam. It felt like Ahmed was a messenger from the town on the sea, and she felt deep emotions rise up inside, but she also struggled to understand why exactly Ahmed was there. He reached into the pockets of his white djellaba and handed the children some sweets.

He looked at Sellass, visibly disturbed.

Sellass did not say a word. She waited for him to speak, her heart pounding. She told the children to go out into the courtyard.

'Sellass,' Ahmed began. 'I went to look for you in Adi Ugri. I made this journey for you, I've been very worried.'

'Do you have news for me?' she asked.

'You can't live here with the children. They're not used to this kind of poverty.'

'Do you have news for me?' Sellass repeated, without a trace of emotion.

'He's trying to leave and he will succeed. He has already made arrangements to board a ship. That's the news, Sellass. It's the truth, I paid good money for it. You will never see him again; he has left the house on the salt flats.'

'You can leave now, Ahmed,' Sellass said in a low voice. 'You shouldn't have come all this way for me. I am fine here with the children, I do not need anything.'

'I have come to tell you that I can provide for you and the children. If you'd like, we can live in Asmara, I have business and a house here. Think of the children, Sellass. They will want for nothing, I will be like a father to them, they will go to school and have a beautiful home.'

'You can leave, Ahmed,' Sellass said again.

'That good-for-nothing.' Ahmed was practically trembling with rage. 'He ruined your life and now he's leaving and will never come back. He'll go and marry an Italian woman. He doesn't care about you – you were just a servant to him – or your children. Just like all the others, you and your bastard children will live out your days in poverty and famine.'

'You can leave, Ahmed.'

He realised that no change had come over her beautiful face, her expression concealed all feeling, a vein pulsed in her long neck.

'Sellass,' he said, cooing her name. 'Ask someone to take care of the children and spend the night with me, just tonight. I will give you so much money that you will be able to buy yourself a house.'

'You can leave, Ahmed,' she said once more, looking at him but without seeing him.

When Ahmed finally left, the children came back inside.

'I remember him,' Marianna proudly said to her mother. 'He used to give me candies when I was with Sinai.'

Sellass stared at her daughter. In that moment, more than ever before, she saw a hint of Carlo in the child's eyes and smile.

'How could he…?' Sellass wondered softly. And then, suddenly, and with great violence, she slapped Marianna. The child was thrown back against the wall. Gianfranco rushed over to his sister's side. For the first time in Marianna's life, she feared her mother. Until then, she had been the centre of her world.

Marianna realised that something terrible had begun.

14

Sellass stopped singing. The lovely songs that she had sung ever since she was a child, long magical tales of enchantment and love, of girls being carried off by the wind to knights who waited for them on mountain tops, were soon nothing but a memory for Marianna and Gianfranco. Sellass had never spoken much but now words weighed heavily inside her. She said only what was essential, together with the question that she muttered to herself each day when she looked at the children, 'How could he…?'

Soon, frown lines appeared on her wide forehead.

In just a few months, it was as if she had aged several years: her cheeks were sunken and her eyebrows were always knitted together in a frown, as if a painful thought afflicted her in one precise spot on her forehead.

She had gone to a local woman to have her hair braided so that she looked like everyone else. She no longer wanted straight hair, the way Carlo had liked it. Now when she went to look for a job, she looked normal. She did not want people thinking she was trying to attract the attention of men so she could sleep with them for money.

She eventually accepted a job in an Italian trattoria, helping out in the kitchen. She realised that she would have to work for the white people if she wanted to feed her children and one day buy a house. It felt like working in a trattoria was better than serving in a family. And at night she could even bring some leftovers back to the children, so they saved money on food.

'I start work tomorrow,' she said one evening to Marianna. 'I'll be gone all day. You'll have to take care of Gianfranco.'

Marianna wanted to cry. It pained her to think that she wouldn't be able to see her mother all day. She still had not got used to that desolate place, so far from all the things that she had loved in her few years of life. When her mother was not there, she felt lost.

'I'm scared you won't come back,' Gianfranco said, his eyes filling with tears. Marianna placed a hand on his small shoulder.

'I'll come back,' Sellass said. 'And I don't want to hear any complaining. I have to work.'

'We can go outside and play with the other children,' Marianna said with enthusiasm. 'There are lots of children outside. Yesterday I saw they had a bicycle rim and were rolling it down the hill.'

'Do whatever you want,' Sellass said with a shrug. 'Just don't make any trouble.'

At dawn, before leaving, she woke up Marianna and greased her long hair with Abyssinian butter and then braided it, so it would stay in place for a few days.

'I won't have time to brush your hair anymore,' she said, handing her a coin. 'Take this to the old lady who sells injera, over near the well, at the end of the street. Ask her for an injera, just one, and share it with Gianfranco.'

'Now?' Marianna asked. She was hungry; they had eaten very little in the past few days.

'Stupid girl! Can't you see it's still dark out?' Sellass said. 'The woman starts making them later, you can go at midday. That's in a few hours, when the sun is high, directly above the courtyard. That's when you go, and no sooner.'

Sellass took off her bracelets and never put them on again; she continued to wear a necklace with a small cross pendant and her earrings. Then she wrapped herself in her futah, covering even her face, and left the house.

It was cold, that piercing cold typical of the high plains, that causes pails of water left outside overnight to freeze.

Marianna lay down next to Gianfranco, pulled the only blanket they had over her head – making her look like a little ball of wool – and went back to sleep.

And then, from far away, the flamingos arrived. Their wings, streaked with pink, glistened in the sky and, for a moment, even concealed the sun. They landed in unison on a golden lake; Marianna saw that even the sea and sky had been dipped in gold. Her father stood on the terrace staring out across the water to where boats and ships bobbed up and down on the waves. Sinai was collecting hermit crabs and laughing and using them to draw shapes on the golden sand: stars, trees and flowers. But then the hermit crabs scuttled off and the stars and flowers disappeared.

When a flamingo approached Marianna, she knew instinctively that she ought to hang on to its slender neck. The flock of birds took flight, climbing higher and higher into the sky. Marianna had never experienced such joy and lightness. She flew through clouds that dissolved into delicate flakes, she felt that all infinity belonged to her, that if she reached out her hand she could touch the sun. Below her lay the vast blue field of the sea, flowering with small boats. Suddenly, she felt herself falling, tumbling into emptiness, she wanted to grab on to something but there was nothing.

Then she saw the kite flying towards her, with its big blue eyes and vermilion lips. It gathered her up as if she were a feather floating through the air, carried along by the wind.

Marianna woke up crying. She never dreamt of her father or of the house in Massawa ever again; slowly those images faded. Only the flamingos returned to her in her sleep, carrying her high up into the sky.

Gianfranco also woke up.

'Can we go outside and play with the other children?' he asked, his voice thick with sleep.

'After we eat. Then we can go play with the other children. Now I have to wait for the sun.' She brushed his hair with her fingers, thinking about how the other children would marvel at his golden curls and green eyes. It was too bad that her braid was a bit greasy, but she'd show the other children how she could walk on her hands, feet in the air; together they'd invent all sorts of games.

Marianna went out into the courtyard and looked up at the sky: the sun was still far away. She saw a few falcons flying between two clouds that resembled sleepy dragons, then walked over to the small bush. She touched the plant's damp leaves and prickly branches. The little birds flew off, chirping in protest. The bush was her friend; she had named him Zubuc. Every day she told him a story, and when she spoke, it looked to her as though his leaves quivered with every word. She was certain that her presence made the bush happy; neither of them had any friends. Marianna stared for a bit at the sun, he had only moved a little, and then she went and sat down in the middle of the courtyard. Gianfranco was sitting on the ground, squashing ants with his fingers, and every so often he looked up at the sun, too.

Marianna stayed very still, clenching the coin her mother had given her in her hand. She wondered why the sun moved so slowly across the sky: clearly he did not care how long she had been waiting. She looked at those distant rays, certain they were the legs of the lord of light; they ought to have carried the light much faster. She stared hard at the sun and invented a silent prayer so he would know she was there. Prayers, Marianna told herself, surely had wings like angels, and could instantly reach even the stars. She felt her eyes burn. Tiny dots of red and gold danced before her, blurring her vision, it felt like the spinning earth was carrying her away. She breathed in deeply and overcame the moment of panic, then opened her eyes and distracted herself by watching the ants. They rushed about, carrying crumbs and bits of straw, never stopping. If the sun had been as fast as the ants were, Marianna thought, she and Gianfranco would have already had their injera. Maybe the sun wasn't moving on purpose; she had been a bad girl, he didn't love her. Maybe he'd never move again, maybe everyone around the world would look up at the sun and wonder why he wasn't moving; they'd never know that it was all because of one little girl. And meanwhile, she'd continue to sit there, waiting pointlessly for him to move, while the ants invaded her body, breaking it down into small crumbs that they'd carry back to their hiding places, deep underground, in the dark. Then, when her mother finally came home, all she'd find in the courtyard would be the coin. She could use it to buy an injera for herself and for Gianfranco. Yes, Marianna would leave her the coin, she thought to herself sadly. Sellass would look for her high and low and call her name and pull out her hair in desperation. But then, when she saw the ants, she would understand. And her grief would last forever, her grief would be as vast as the sky in which the sun sat without moving.

'Marianna!' Gianfranco yelled. 'Look, the sun is high,' he said, pointing at the sky. She looked up. So, the sun had decided to surprise her while she was thinking about ants and now he stood high above the courtyard.

'I'm going,' she said, holding the coin tightly in her hand.

'I want to come, too,' Gianfranco whined, preferring not to be left alone. 'I'll squash the other ants later on.'

'You shouldn't squash them,' she said sternly. 'They have homes and children waiting for them.'

They set out to go and see Elsa, the elderly woman who cooked injera. No one knew exactly why she had an Italian name. She had patchy tufts of white hair, which she tried to keep in place with a strip of red fabric; she was small, skinny and had long bony feet that stuck out from her dress; her fingers were long, too, and her hands were so wrinkled and black they looked like they had been parched by the sun. She blew under the *mogogo* to rekindle the fire, poured the batter in the pan and muttered to herself as the injera cooked.

Marianna stepped forward timidly, holding her brother's hand. While walking there, she had noticed how everyone had stared at them but no one had smiled or waved. People's faces had been hostile, closed, withdrawn.

'Are you Sellass' children?' the woman asked while continuing to mix the batter.

'Yes,' Marianna replied. 'We have money for an injera,' she said, handing the woman her coin.

Elsa placed the coin in a pocket of her dress, poured some batter into the pan, sat down on a stool and looked at the children quietly.

'*Bei bambini*,' she said warmly in Italian, then started talking to herself softly. 'Don't play outside,' she added. 'People around here are bad. I'll make you a very big injera, no one makes them as good as I do.'

'Why are the people bad?' Marianna asked, sidling up to the woman; she immediately felt a kinship with her, both for the way she had spoken to them and because of her brightly coloured floral dress.

Elsa shrugged. 'You're better off staying at home. People around here are... different from us.'

'How are they different?' Marianna asked.

'They're Habesha,' the woman said, sliding the injera off the griddle.

'Why is your name "Elsa"?'

'Like you, I have an Italian name,' the old woman said with a smile, showing her toothless gums. 'An Italian man named me Elsa. I used to live in the centre of Asmara. Then I got old and everyone died, but not me, I will never die. That's why I make injera here. And when death comes for me, I'll make her an injera, too. A big one.'

Gianfranco stared at Elsa, his eyes open wide in amazement.

'Crazy old lady,' Elsa laughed. 'I'm just a crazy old lady who loves children like you two,' she said and patted

Gianfranco's head, mumbling God's name over and over. 'Now, hurry on home because others will soon arrive to buy their injera. And tomorrow come a little later so we can talk some more.'

The children went home to their courtyard to eat their injera.

The little birds sat on the bush staring eagerly at the crumbs that fell on the ground. Then Marianna and Gianfranco went outside to watch the children play. Some of them, the very smallest ones, their heads almost completely shaven except for one dark lock in the middle, ran after the older children, falling down frequently but getting right back up. Marianna and Gianfranco stood off to one side and watched as they rolled a rusty bicycle rim along the ground.

A little boy came up to them. 'What do you want?' he asked unkindly.

'We want to play with you,' Marianna said. 'We live over there.'

'I know where you live,' the boy said. 'You're mulattos. We don't want you here.' Other children came running over. They also stared unkindly at Marianna and Gianfranco.

'Mulattos!' one of the children shouted and soon all the others chimed in. 'Dirty mulattos! Mulattos!' they shouted.

A woman stood watching from the doorway of her tukul, cleaning her teeth with a piece of tree bark.

Gianfranco started to cry, Marianna squeezed his hand, and then someone pushed her and she fell to the ground, bringing her brother down with her. The children then started to pull Gianfranco's hair and kick Marianna in the face and up and down her back, laughing and yelling the whole time.

An old shepherd passing by with his goats rushed over and chased the children away, waving his staff and threatening to hit them.

Marianna and Gianfranco were in tears, their clothes were torn and their faces were scratched.

'Where do you live?' the shepherd asked.

Marianna pointed at their house and stopped crying. She wanted to show the old man that she was strong.

'Go home,' the old man said. 'I'll wait here until you're inside.'

The woman in the doorway continued to watch and did not stop cleaning her teeth. Other women joined her, they all stood together, looking at the children and shepherd with indifference. The children snickered and laughed from afar.

The shepherd turned towards the women, waved his staff in the air and spat forcefully onto the ground.

Once they were back inside, Marianna tried to soothe Gianfranco, who kept crying for his mother; she told him about the birds with the pink feathers and the old kite, how it slept high up in the faraway palm tree, and eventually he fell asleep.

Marianna waited anxiously for her mother to come home. It was worse waiting at night than during the day, because at least during the day she had sunlight.

She was scared and felt immensely lonely. At each and every sound she got up and ran to the door, hoping it was her mother, but beyond the threshold was only darkness; the shadows had erased the entire village, leaving only the cry of the hyenas.

Marianna tried hard to think of something that would distract her from the pitch-black night, as its darkness made her fear terrible things. Every shadow hid unknown faces, and each sound of footsteps could be someone coming to take them away.

When Sellass finally came home, Marianna felt her anxiety about the night disappear, as if a great number of lights had suddenly been turned on.

Sellass took off her futah and nodded at the children in greeting. Gianfranco rushed over and grabbed handfuls of her skirt while she put a bundle of food down on the table. Marianna was excited by the prospect of food, and it looked like a lot; the injera had quelled her hunger only for a few minutes.

Then Gianfranco told his mother about what happened to them earlier in the day and showed her the bruise on his arm.

Marianna would have preferred not to say anything, as she didn't want to upset Sellass, but she had to answer her questions and even utter the word 'mulatto.'

Their mother sat on the side of the bed, head in her hands. Then she stood up, grabbed Marianna, shook her hard several times and slapped her.

'You mustn't go looking for trouble! And don't take your brother outside with you,' she said without raising her voice. 'Or else I'll leave you in a place that you'll never get out of. I won't let you ruin my life, too.'

Marianna started to cry while Gianfranco sat there quietly, sucking his thumb and biting his fingernails.

Marianna went to bed and pulled the blanket over her head.

She was desperately unhappy. Her mother had changed so much, as if one of those cruel men from Sinai's stories had cast a spell on her. She and Gianfranco were not allowed to play with the other children because they were mulatto. That word had wounded her, it clearly meant something terrible, just like that other word that Mebrat had used: 'bastards.'

Everything had been so different back in Massawa, in the house by the sea.

If only the ants had devoured Marianna while she was waiting for the sun to climb high into the sky. Then her mother would've regretted hitting her and felt bad about loving Gianfranco more, she would've wept and called out for Marianna, saying her name over and over. But Marianna would never have returned.

15

The following day, Marianna took Gianfranco to buy injera. She combed his hair with her fingers, proud that Elsa had admired his locks.

Once again, she spent the morning sitting in the courtyard for hours without moving. She thought that sitting still was an important part of the ritual, that the sun would climb faster if she did. Holding her coin tightly, she let her mind wander, her eyes on the swooping falcons overhead; there were so many of them, so many commas set between clusters of words composed by the clouds high up in the sky. She also carefully observed the birds who visited Zubuc: small and lively, with multicoloured feathers. They hopped and cheeped in their expressive language, constantly changing their tone. Zubuc was very patient and put up with all their noise. In moments like that, the plant felt no different from his brethren who lived in totally different kinds of gardens. When the sun finally reached his zenith, Marianna bowed, wanting to stay on his good side, hoping to build a bond of friendship that rose up from the courtyard into the clear azure sky, so the sun would move faster with each passing day.

In the meantime, after destroying entire cities of ants, Gianfranco had started building roads and bridges for them, hoping to give the busy little creatures something far grander. But the tiny ants carefully avoided the new structures, searching in vain for their old paths and crevices.

Elsa greeted them in Italian and called them 'bei bambini' once more.

'I heard that the children hit and kicked you yesterday,' she said, gently caressing Marianna's forehead with her calloused hand. 'Last night I went over and yelled at them; they're afraid of me,' she said, giving them a gummy smile.

Marianna smiled back, happy to have found a friend and ally.

'Are you hungry, children?' Elsa asked, stirring the batter.

'Yes, I am,' Marianna replied. 'Gianfranco is hardly ever hungry. In Massawa I had a friend, whose name was Sinai, who used to call him little bird because he ate so little. But today even Gianfranco asked why the sun was so slow.'

Elsa didn't understand what Marianna meant so the girl explained how they had to wait for the sun to be high in the sky.

'Don't stand there waiting for him,' Elsa said gravely, as if sharing precious advice with the child. 'The sun knows what he has to do, and he knows you by now. He won't let you down. When the rains come, you might not even see him for a while, but the dark clouds will pass and he will return.'

'When will the rains come?'

'In a few months. And then it will be much cooler. I have an old heart that waits for the rain the same way you wait for the sun,' Elsa said, placing a hand on her chest. Marianna noticed that she wore a thin gold band set with a pretty shiny stone on one of her fingers.

'They called us "mulatto,"' Marianna said, remembering her pressing question. Maybe Elsa would be able to explain what that word meant.

Gianfranco stood silently watching sparks from the burning wood rise slowly into the sky, mesmerised by those small momentary worlds of fire.

'There's nothing bad about being mulatto,' Elsa said. 'On the contrary, you're lucky that you have a white father and black mother, it means you're both, a mix. Let me tell you a story: when God made the first man, he mixed together the ingredients the same way I mix my teff, but when he was cooking up his creation, it started to rain and the fire went out, so the man came out too white. Then God tried again but he got distracted because he always has so many things to do and he left his creation on the fire for too long, so the next man came out burnt and black. The time after that God was very careful and his creation was just the right colour, a mix between black and white.'

Marianna smiled widely, proud to be just the right colour. How lucky they had been to meet Elsa, she thought. Although she was as black as the burnt man, she had turned out good anyway.

Two women came to buy injera, paid for them and then hurried out, without even glancing at the children.

While Marianna and Gianfranco were walking home, the children who had attacked them reappeared.

'Mulatto, mulatto,' they taunted them, 'We don't want mulatto kids here.'

One of the boys, the oldest, yanked on Marianna's braid. Another child kicked her. Then they both pushed Gianfranco, who fell down. When Marianna saw her brother on the ground, crying, the children pulling his hair, mussing it up, she felt something new come over her: a burst of terrible rage, a force she had never felt before. She bent down, picked up a rock and rushed over to the oldest boy. She was breathing hard and her cheeks were on fire, as if she had a fever. She looked into his eyes – he suddenly seemed scared – and hit him on the head with the stone. His scream echoed throughout Edaga Arbi; when he brought his hand to his head, blood started to run down his face. The other children ran back to their tukuls and the women came out to see what was going on.

'Let's go,' Marianna said, taking Gianfranco's hand. 'No one will ever beat us up again. They're just nasty Habesha.'

She started running, pulling her brother along with her. In the meantime, he had stopped crying and looked up at Marianna with admiration. When they reached the house, he wiped his runny nose on his sister's sleeve.

Sellass arrived home late. To Marianna it felt like those evening hours before her mother returned were endless. Fearing that someone might come in and beat them up for what she had done, she dragged her angareb up to the door to block it.

They had just finished eating dinner when there was a knock on the door. Marianna felt her heart pounding in her chest, but when she opened the door she stayed calm. It was a woman, she was holding the wounded child by the hand, and she stared at Marianna with deep bitterness. Other women and children stood behind her.

The woman entered the house and walked towards Sellass. 'Your daughter cracked my son's skull. Look at his wound! Haile says that he might become very ill if we don't get him the right medicine, it's a serious wound.'

The boy looked up at Sellass and Marianna innocently, every so often bringing his hand to the slightly dirty bandage, a rag that had been haphazardly tied around his head. His aggressive manner had disappeared entirely, he looked like a little black angel, with big dark eyes and a sad smile on his full mouth.

Sellass looked at the child's head for a moment without saying anything.

'Put a clean bandage on it instead of that old rag,' she eventually said in a soft but decisive manner. 'What do you want from me? Money? So that you can take him to the doctor... or for something else? It doesn't look serious to me,' she said, then went to get a couple of coins and threw them at the woman's feet.

'If it happens again,' the boy's mother said, bending down to pick up the coins, 'you'll be in big trouble. Keep your bastard children inside.'

'Leave,' Sellass said, 'and don't worry. My children will never go near your children ever again. I don't want them to have anything to do with street kids. And besides, your children attacked them first.'

A choir of protests rose up from the other women but Sellass slammed the door shut on them.

Marianna was sitting down on the angareb next to Gianfranco. Her mother walked over, grabbed her arm, and made her stand up. She then stared at her daughter silently for a few moments, noting again that the expression in Marianna's eyes was just like Carlo's. They also both clenched their lips firmly together when something worried them. She let go of the child, slapped her several times, then pushed her down onto the floor, hard. She could not stop herself and would have continued if Gianfranco had not grabbed her skirt and started crying.

From where she huddled on the ground, Marianna gasped for air and covered her head with her arms. Then she started crying: a long and subdued wail that seemed like it would never end.

'No more going out to buy injera,' Sellass said quietly. 'No more going out ever again. I don't want any more trouble than I already have. You're not going to ruin my life, do you understand me?'

Marianna tried thinking about the sun and about Elsa, but nothing could console her. Even Zubuc, sitting out there in the dark, was oblivious to her pain and remained fast asleep, all covered in dewdrops. Marianna felt sad, infinitely alone, and lost in a dark and unfamiliar world. And yet, she could not stop loving her mother.

16

Carlo, together with other Italian prisoners, was forced to board a ship for South Africa, where he would then be transported to a prison camp. The harbour area was charged with tension. Gone were the days when ships arrived from Italy filled with men ready to build an empire. That empire had been crushed, along with all hopes for it.

The English soldiers – tall, brisk, austere – issued their orders sharply and perfunctorily. The ship had to leave Massawa as quickly as possible.

Relatives of the prisoners were not allowed on the pier, they had to stand at a distance and could only watch, tears in their eyes, as their loved ones were sent to their sad destinies. People sobbed, cries of anguish and words of encouragement were called out. Some people tried to remain calm and smile with restraint and wave their farewells.

Meanwhile, on the wharf, local men furtively shook hands with some of the prisoners, softly wishing them well and asking God to bless and protect them.

When the boat left the harbour, Carlo, who was on deck with everyone else, waiting to be separated into groups, did not turn to look back at Massawa as it receded into the distance. He had not slept for three nights and now, after the anxiety of the most recent hours, he was overcome by a terrible fatigue. He just wanted to lie down, fall asleep and forget, at least temporarily, the nightmare of war and the unknowable hell that lay ahead of him. He heard voices inside his head: Sellass, the children, the bleating of the goat when he returned to the house in the evening, the repetitive chanting of the Eritrean labourers as they toiled. None of the faces around him were familiar. The men were from Asmara, Keren, Dekemhare, and of all ages. Many wore the desperate look of having left everything behind, realising only then just how much they had loved it all, carrying memories of people dear to them, people who had also been abandoned to uncertainty and anguish.

A feeling of intense despair hung heavily in the humidity, as if the world had awoken with an intolerably painful wound, and it intended to inflict the resulting suffering on its creatures.

The ship picked up steam and headed out to open sea.

Through the mist of sleep which he was unable to fend off any longer, Carlo saw his mother. She was lighting a fire, it was November, the first foggy days of the year. He listened to the men as they told their war stories; such tales had always filled him with fear, ever since he was a child. And yet he was convinced that he would never actually witness battle. Through the thick fog he caught sight of a few trees and their last coppery leaves, he heard the river rush by. Then, swirling high up in the sky, he saw the pink wings of the flamingos, the birds with the long slender necks came from afar, the fog lifted, and suddenly he could clearly see their outstretched wings in the light.

'Mr. Carlo Cinzi?' A British soldier stood before him. Carlo took note of the man's young age, his blue eyes, his immature gaze.

'Mr. Carlo Cinzi?' the soldier repeated. This time Carlo seemed to detect a hint of kindness and understanding. He nodded and thought back to his interrogation, to the English officer with the red moustache who had been so arrogant and gruff with him, as if he had been the weakest man on the losing side.

In the early days of the journey, Carlo met some of his fellow prisoners and they exchanged a few words to bolster each other. Sometimes all it took was a glance or a kind word to make their days more tolerable. Many had left wives and children behind. With a mixture of both pain and pride, some even shared photographs of them.

Among the people Carlo met – in a strange twist of fate – was the husband of the lovely red-haired young lady whom he had encountered on his initial journey to Africa. He was an elegant man, spoke in a soft voice, and even occasionally managed to obtain a few cigarettes, which seemed to be his main goal in life. He had shown his wife's photograph around and that was how Carlo had recognised, with some amazement, Signorina Giuliana, the first-class passenger.

There was an attractive young woman on board this ship, too. Occasionally she was accompanied by a child, a pretty girl with long blond braids. Carlo discovered the woman was Italian, the second wife of an English officer; when she crossed paths with the soldiers, she always greeted them with a courteous nod and a shy smile. The little girl was often on deck; whenever she saw a school of dolphins swimming and playing alongside the ship, she would turn to look at the men to see if anyone else was enjoying the spectacle. When Carlo looked at the blond child, he felt his heart ache with nostalgia for a serenity that he would never know again, for the laughter and games and joy of a world that was now lost to him.

The ship left the Red Sea and entered the Indian Ocean.

The ocean was calm, the water was a deep dark blue, without any hint of azure.

Carlo was in the infirmary having a finger wound treated when a sudden massive explosion caused the entire ship to tremble and immediately list to one side. It was as if the world had exploded into space: everything fell about, and the sound was so loud it echoed through the heavens.

A Japanese submarine had torpedoed the ship, striking the cargo section. There was a moment of quiet and then, from all directions, came the sound of yelling, pleading, praying.

Carlo managed to rush out of the infirmary and make his way on deck. He realised that there was no time to lower the lifeboats, the boat was about to sink. It seemed impossible that a craft as massive as theirs, which only a moment earlier had been travelling swiftly across the water, was now a negligible object about to be swallowed up by the ocean.

Carlo refused to accept that he was destined to disappear into the depths of that night-coloured ocean, so indifferent to the men who flailed about in its waves, struggling to survive.

A knot of desperation filled his throat. He tried to talk to himself but his voice had vanished, as if it had already come face to face with death. It was just a nightmare, he told himself, soon he'd wake up and realise that it was all a dream. He couldn't possibly die, he was too young, barely into his thirties.

He was still on board the sinking ship — his thoughts lasted a second but felt endless — when he saw the young Englishman in the water, trying to help a fellow soldier.

Carlo dove in to assist them, but the two young men disappeared below the water. He managed to reach a large piece of wood, which some other men were holding on to; many other objects bobbed about on the waves.

'Help them!' he heard someone shout.

The young Italian woman cried out in desperation, trying to save her daughter. A soldier swam towards them, but the woman was much farther away than she appeared. The child let go and vanished beneath the surface. Shortly afterwards, waves rippled over where the woman had once been.

And then the sharks appeared, as if a manifestation of the horror of it all. Their dark rigid fins headed straight to the men who kicked and splashed, trying to find something they could grab on to that would hold them up.

Carlo watched the fins as if hypnotised. It occurred to him that it was a Wednesday, but he wasn't entirely certain. The voices of the men around him turned into a collective scream of desperation, filling the air. Attracted by the vibrations transmitted through the water, the sharks came darting towards them. Carlo held on to the board as tightly as possible, until his hands hurt. The screams of the dying entered his brain, exploding into tiny splinters. He looked up at the sky, hoping to catch sight of some mysterious signal that would alleviate his terror. He saw the three seagulls that had been following the ship for much of the journey. They descended lower and lower, skimming the surface of the water to reach the flagpole, where they had often rested, now fast disappearing. Their wings shone brightly in the sunlight.

Carlo heard someone shout his name. It was Signorina Giuliana's husband. He was trying to reach the piece of wood. Carlo looked away so as not to see him drown; he did not move, his hands had become claws, he would never let go.

Then came a sensation of indifference: he felt removed from the horror that surrounded him, as if suddenly detached from reality and merely a duplicate of himself. A man nearby started to weep.

When the ocean closed over the ship, there was the sustained sound of splashing waves, followed by silence.

17

Elsa owned a small house just outside Ghezzabanda, a neighbourhood of Asmara where many Italians lived. When her day in Edaga Arbi ended, she made her way home by foot. She watered the flowers in her small garden and then sat on the stoop; she enjoyed resting there at sunset, watching the fiery colours quickly give way to the evening.

Elsa went to Edaga Arbi to make injera because it was a way of feeling useful, of being with people. She couldn't conceive of spending the entire day at home, waiting for her life on this earth to end.

She had left her village at the age of fourteen after a swarm of locusts had destroyed her family's crops, leaving her parents destitute and desperate, unable to feed their nine children and the elders of the family. Elsa, whose name at the time was Haimanot, moved to Asmara in the hopes of finding work.

It was 1900, and in those days Asmara was still a small village with few Europeans.

Elsa found work in the home of an Italian engineer who had arrived in Asmara only a few months earlier. A man of about fifty, he had an imposing manner and genteel ways. A boy named Negasc kept house for him and seemed very loyal. Haimanot was asked to live in the house and work for the engineer as his washerwoman. She would have to learn how to iron, but Eritrean girls learnt new tasks and the new language very quickly. The engineer decided to call her Elsa because he couldn't be bothered to pronounce Haimanot.

Elsa was beautiful: she had the delicate features of a black Madonna, a broad smile and white teeth. Despite being petite and slender, she was very strong and always returned from the market with a large basket on top of her head. Whenever she saw il Signor *ingegnere*, she kept her eyes downcast as he seemed to be a very important man.

One day Negasc told her that the engineer was going through a difficult time: he had many worries and spent most of his evenings sitting in his armchair, pondering his troubles and drinking. Sometimes he even said that he hoped to return to Italy.

Elsa slept in a tiny bedroom in the courtyard, large enough only for an angareb and a small lamp. One night, just after she had fallen asleep, she heard someone knocking on the door. She got very scared. Then she heard the engineer's voice.

'Elsa,' the man said gently, 'open the door.'

When the engineer walked in, she could smell alcohol and tobacco on his breath. A strange feeling came over her, filling her with warmth. He was wearing a silk bathrobe and in the shadows he looked like a giant with silver hair.

'Come, sit down, Elsa,' the engineer whispered and pulled her towards him on the angareb. He said some other words but she did not understand them. Then he took off her clothes. Elsa felt his trembling hands caress her body. She felt both fear and pleasure, her head was spinning, his hands made her feel very warm deep inside, where her heart had often felt fear. She had always admired il Signor ingegnere, but she did not understand why he had decided to come to visit her, a young black girl who did his laundry, and moreover at night. Maybe alcohol had clouded his thoughts.

The engineer returned to her room regularly. When Elsa opened the door and smelt his breath, a scent she came to love, her heart beat fast and her skin burned and tingled.

When Elsa became pregnant, the engineer sent her back to her village with some money and told her to let him know when the child was born.

She gave birth to a beautiful baby girl with skin the colour of the moon. Elsa was almost afraid to touch her, fearing she would ruin the child's beauty.

The engineer seemed very happy when he saw the infant, he gently touched her head and observed her in silence.

Elsa stayed on in the village with her daughter. She lacked for nothing because the engineer gave her money, which she used to help her parents and relatives. The family was forced to accept the situation after the engineer came to the village, greeting the elders with respect and handing sweets to all the children.

When the little girl turned one, the engineer, who came to visit her every month, told Elsa that he had to return to Italy and that he wanted to take his daughter with him. He would see to her education, she would grow up in a beautiful home in a large Italian city, she would be well off and well educated. In exchange, he would buy Elsa a home in Asmara and send her news of the child. It was a difficult decision for Elsa to make and she cried a great deal, knowing she would never see il Signor ingegnere again, but she also was aware that her beautiful, fair-skinned daughter, who resembled her father so much, would, in this way, have a future in the distant land of the white people, a future that she could never have either in the small village or in Asmara. The engineer also said that if Elsa didn't give him the child, he would leave her without a penny. Clearly he wanted the child very much. Staring down at her daughter, Elsa realised that if she were to keep her, the most she could grow up to become would be a servant, whereas a child as delicate and luminous as she, who seemed to have been sent there by heaven, was destined to become a great lady.

And so it was that, one day, the engineer left with little Maria Cristina and a nun, who accompanied them on the long journey to take care of the child.

Elsa stayed on in her village for some time. Every day she walked to a distant valley, sat down on a large boulder, rested her head on her knee and cried. Thinking of her daughter and il Signor ingegnere, her frail body shuddered with violent sobs.

The valley and dry hills echoed with the voice of the wind, the call of rapacious birds and Elsa's sorrow. She wanted to sit on the boulder forever, or be transformed into a clod of earth and never feel pain, or become a bird with giant wings and fly all the way to where Maria Cristina and il Signor ingegnere lived.

Then Elsa stopped crying. Gaunt and sad, she returned to Asmara. She found a new job as a washerwoman in an Italian family who treated her well but gave her a great deal of work; she spent her days hunched over the washboard cleaning mountains of things.

She rented a small house. All she needed was an angareb to sleep on.

A year later, the priest brought her a short letter, which he read to her, and a photograph of Maria Cristina. In the photo, the child wore a long white frock and a large straw hat; she had dark curly hair and was sitting on a chair in a garden with numerous trees and a fountain; next to her was a woman wearing a white dress and a nurse's cap.

The engineer wrote that the woman in the picture, Signorina Teresa, cared for the child with great affection.

Two years later, Elsa received a second letter, another photograph and some money. Again Maria Cristina was dressed in white, but this time she was at the seaside, laughing. The engineer wrote that everything was fine, the child was well behaved, intelligent and happy.

Elsa left her job as a washerwoman and went to work for an Italian couple in the centre of Asmara. She was happy there, she learnt how to cook, soon became very adept at it, and the family was pleased with her.

Elsa liked both the lady of the house, an early coloniser who wore a thick braid in a crown on her head, and her husband, who spoke little and was always a bit gruff but a kind man overall.

She worked for them for almost twenty years. Shortly after the lady of the house died, her husband died too.

Elsa did not want to work for any more families. She retreated into her little home, planted white flowers in her garden, and named each one of them after Maria Cristina. When vendors came to her gate to offer their wares and admire her flowers, Elsa would say, 'These are all my Maria Cristinas,' and the vendors would walk away, shaking their heads at her strange manner.

Over the years, other letters and three photographs arrived. One of the most recent showed a beautiful girl standing in front of a large arch; she was tall, slender and wore a light-coloured dress and large hat that shaded her face. Elsa detected something of the engineer in her, but the girl's smile, Elsa noticed with a touch of pride, was all hers.

One morning, while Elsa was in church, kneeling down and praying, the priest came towards her with a letter. Elsa saw right away that the handwriting was different. The letter had been written by a lawyer who was informing her of the death of the engineer, who had left a will with his final wishes. He did not want Maria Cristina to be informed of her mother's existence in Asmara. For the girl's wellbeing, and in order not to create any emotional conflicts, she had always been told that her mother had died during childbirth. Maria Cristina had gone on to become a doctor, she worked in a hospital, and she was very successful. Her only sadness was the loss of her father, whom she had adored. No one would write to Elsa again with news of her daughter, but she could rest easy: Maria Cristina was a very fortunate woman.

Elsa cried when she looked at the final photograph, but then felt a touch of happiness when she noticed how impressed the priest was by Maria Cristina, and in particular that she had gone on to become a doctor.

She was a true lady, Elsa remarked to herself, looking at the young woman. It was right that she should not learn anything about her mother; after all she was only a poor servant who signed her name with an X.

In the past, she had nurtured hopes that the engineer and her daughter would one day make a trip to Asmara and she would finally be able to see the beautiful girl with the fair skin, to whom she had given birth in a small mountain village.

For that particular occasion, she had even had some dentures made; an infection in her gums had caused all her teeth to fall out and she didn't want Maria Cristina to see her toothless smile. After receiving the final letter, though, she put the dentures away.

The idea of an encounter with il Signor ingegnere and her grown daughter had come to Elsa in a dream. She had seen Maria Cristina come dancing towards her down the streets of Asmara in a dress that rippled lightly around her like a cloud, and tossing flowers to her mother; there had been the sound of leaves fluttering through the air.

Elsa decided to spend the rest of her days making injera in Edaga Arbi. The priest had said that it would help others and herself, it would take her out of her house, where she spent her time watching the hours go by.

And so, each day, she made the journey to and from that faraway neighbourhood filled with many poor women and their children, just to make injera. She sold them to beggars for a penny and always cooked extra, which she gave away. She would stay there a few hours, talking to people. Some folks needed someone to talk to, while others just wanted company and stood there without making a sound, watching her stir her batter and cook.

When Elsa saw the mixed-race girl and her brother, she was filled with sadness. She thanked God that her daughter had been taken far away from the misery in which they lived.

The sight of the little boy with big green eyes and blond curls was particularly troubling: he looked like one of the angels on the ceiling of the cathedral where she went to pray each day.

Gazing upon Marianna, all sorts of memories came flooding back to her and filled her head: the way il Signor ingegnere had looked at her, the time they had spent together, the way Maria Cristina's skin had smelt like milk, her daughter's copper-coloured hair.

She had eagerly waited for the mixed-race girl to return for injera so that she could peer deep into her eyes, observe her manner, and discover something else that reminded her of her own daughter, whom she had only been able to enjoy for a year. But Marianna and her brother never came back. Nor did Elsa ever see Sellass again, that proud woman who walked through the village with her face covered, passing like a shadow across the earth.

Elsa heard about the boy who had been wounded, the local women had told her that the incident had been caused by the mulatto children – some said one thing, others said something else.

One evening, while sitting on the step outside her house and admiring her Maria Cristinas, feeling rejuvenated by the first heavy rains of the season, Elsa decided that the following day she would go and look for the two children.

18

Marianna sat on a straw mat in the middle of the room, staring at the shiny thread that hung down from the ceiling. A spider rotated around it, spinning a light and translucent web it would use to catch its prey. Marianna spent hours observing the spider at work, careful not to disturb the lengthy process, and when the web was ready, she waited for the spider to catch an insect. She even instructed her little brother to be careful not to destroy the spider's creation. Gianfranco, meanwhile, rolled a balled-up piece of paper back and forth, stopping only to let it dry if it happened to roll through one of the puddles on the floor. Rain had poured through the holes in the roof.

Marianna's hair was messy – a few days had passed since her mother had done her braid – her dress was wrinkled, and she wore cardboard shoes, tied with pieces of string.

Someone knocked on the door. Marianna was always fearful that something awful would happen on the long days when her mother was out of the house.

'It's me, Elsa,' the woman called out.

Marianna, pleased by the surprise, ran to open the door.

She had often thought about the woman who made injera, and how kind she had been with them.

'I brought you an injera,' Elsa said, standing in the doorway. 'Why didn't you ever come back?'

'I don't have money to pay you for it,' Marianna said, glancing towards the sun, recalling the mornings she had spent waiting to go to see Elsa.

'I don't want you to pay me for it. I brought it for you and your little brother.'

They sat on the broken step outside the front door. Marianna told herself that she was still obeying her mother and had not let anyone in. She called Gianfranco over to sit with them.

'Elsa, you grew teeth!' Marianna exclaimed, after peering at her carefully.

A great big smile spread across Elsa's dark face.

Even Gianfranco was amazed. To verify the existence of Elsa's new teeth, he wanted to touch one of them.

'Aren't they wonderful?' the woman said with great pleasure. 'I found them there one morning when I woke up. I suppose it's because I watered my mouth every day for a long time. And on Sundays I even give it a glass of *mies*,' she said, laughing heartily, small wrinkles forming an intricate pattern around her eyes. It was the first time she had put in the dentures, she hadn't even worn them to talk to the priest. Wearing them now made her feel as though they hadn't been a waste of money after all.

'You look very pretty,' Marianna said, touching her bright green dress and nodding at the ribbon of the same colour meant to control Elsa's frizzy patches of white hair.

'You should water your head, too!' Gianfranco said, enthusiastically.

'I tried, but my hair just doesn't want to grow.'

A mangy stray dog with a stumpy tail and scabs on its back came and lay down at Elsa's feet. He sniffed the air and looked at the children. Even though he was dirty and hungry, he seemed happy to have found some friends. He was also unexpectedly fortunate: Gianfranco offered him a piece of his injera that he had eyed on arrival.

Elsa told the children amusing stories to make them smile and promised that one day she would take them around Asmara, after asking their mother's permission, of course.

Following Elsa's departure and countless hugs and kisses goodbye, Marianna did not return to her spider but instead went to see Zubuc, who was in grand form due to all the rain. Shiny drops sparkled like diamonds on his small leaves. The bush, decked out as if for a party, inhaled the moist air. The birds, who had been forced to hide in small holes in the ground because of the thunder, soon flew back to his branches and started shaking them again.

When evening arrived, Marianna stretched out on the ground, ear to the soil. It felt like she could see her mother leave her place of work and begin her journey home to Edaga Arbi. Marianna counted her steps. Listening very carefully, she thought she could hear her approaching. One hundred steps, then another hundred steps to the shops owned by the Indians, then another hundred steps to the grain market, then the path that led to the beginning of the climb uphill, which was more or less another couple of hundred steps, then a few more hundred to cross the village and finally reach their doorstep. Tum-tum, tum-tum, she heard her mother's footsteps echoing deep in the earth, and she continued to count. She could see Sellass striding through the darkness.

Marianna had learnt to count in Massawa, using small pebbles she found on the beach. She used to build circles with them and then watch as waves washed over them, a game she used to play with the sea back when she still didn't know what it meant to be afraid.

While Marianna lay on the ground counting steps, Gianfranco slept, forbidden from interrupting the ritual which would end with his mother's return.

Then, all of a sudden, heavy dark clouds, swollen with water and crashing into each other like a herd of crazed sheep, raced across the sky; there was thunder and lightning and the rain beat down violently on their poor dwelling.

Marianna got to her feet. Rain came pouring in through the holes in the roof, creating large puddles on the ground. She dragged an angareb over to the one dry corner and anxiously went to check on the spiderweb. First she saw it fluttering in a gust of wind that blew through the window – part of the cardboard panel had fallen out – then she saw it waft down into a puddle on the ground, where it got tangled into a knot of threads. Marianna looked around for the spider, but it had disappeared. To stop herself from thinking about the thunder, she carried a sleeping Gianfranco over to the angareb and took off his wet trousers. The child did not even wake up, he just kept on sucking his thumb. Marianna lay down next to him and tried to remember where she was with the counting of the steps, how many she had skipped.

Just then Sellass walked in. She was soaking wet.

She quickly removed her futah, dried her face, and put the bag with the food down on the dry angareb. Marianna watched her. She was glad her mother was home and tried to detect some of the day's labours on her face. Gianfranco woke up and immediately started biting the sleeve of his old sweater, tugging at the threads with his teeth.

'Eat,' Sellass said. She opened the bag and flopped down on the angareb. She looked at the puddles on the floor and the piece of cardboard that had fallen out of the window frame. Her expression was always the same, no matter what. No emotions ever etched their way across her dark, stony face; her large dark eyes were opaque shadowy mirrors.

'I took off Gianfranco's wet trousers,' Marianna said softly, afraid of interrupting her mother, whose attention was elsewhere.

Sellass gripped the frame of the angareb.

Every night when she came home, she felt the overpowering urge to beat and insult Marianna. She tried hard to control herself but often did not succeed. A savage force exploded inside her head like a hurricane and was placated only when Marianna started to cry. Later in the night, lying down, she felt a dull ache fill her chest. She tried to forget how hard their life had become, her daughter's sobs, the face of the man she saw in Marianna.

As Sellass waited for sleep to come, she tried to find a single element of solace. She thought of the money she kept hidden away and how one day she would use it to buy them a house.

19

Tedla the Crazy travelled through imaginary lands, talking and laughing to himself. No one knew where he actually came from; he had always lived on the streets of Asmara. At night he slept in a shack near the main church, people gave him food, and a young priest occasionally called him inside for a bowl of soup. He wore rags blackened with time, had long hair, and walked with a stick. 'He has always looked the same,' people used to say, as if he had never been a child and would never grow old. Tedla was safe in his own world, outside of time. One night he left his shack near the church and went to sleep in the Coptic graveyard because he had heard people say – sometimes a light came on in his head and he understood the world around him – that a pack of hyenas had dug up some of the dead and ripped their bodies to shreds.

Meret, the vegetable seller in Asmara, was particularly upset to learn about the hyenas. She let everyone know that her mother had recently been buried there and that now she herself was having nightmares. Meret cried as she described her dreams: her mother screaming for her daughter, the hyenas dragging her out of her final resting place, flaying her body and howling in the darkness. Beating her chest, Meret said that if such a thing ever came to pass, her mother's spirit would wander in desperation forever, begging for the suffering to end.

Tedla strode angrily up and down the streets of Asmara, waving his stick in the air and yelling at no one in particular, and then made his way to the cemetery to look for a shack where he could sleep at night and chase away the hyenas, in case they returned. He arrived at the burial ground at dark and lay down in a freshly dug grave, covering his head with rags so that sleep would come to him. He went on to tell everyone he met that he slept in the place of the dead to keep away the hyenas. When a priest found out, he tried to convince Tedla not to return to the graves, he told him that the hyenas had left, that they had gone to sleep in caves which they would never leave.

Tedla had always had great respect for the priests, so he let himself be convinced, but he did not want to go back to sleeping in the shack near the church; a strange fear of the city streets where he had spent his entire life had since come over him. So he walked and walked in total silence, as if all the words that had kept him company in the daytime hours had now been extinguished. Eventually he reached the outskirts of Edaga Arbi.

It was sunset when he encountered the procession of beggars on their return to their poor dwellings. He joined them, giving the coins he carried in a pouch on his belt to a blind man, and chose a spot to sleep not far from the donkey and goat pen.

He never left Edaga Arbi again. In a matter of days, Tedla the Crazy grew into a pensive and wizened old man, as if time, after ignoring him for so long while he lived on the streets of Asmara, quickly caught up with him. First his hair and beard turned white, then his face wrinkled up like a fruit dried out by the sun, and finally his whole body began to tremble.

In a new state of calm of both body and mind, Tedla sat staring out at the infinite sky for hours on end. He used his stick, which lay at his feet, only to make his way back to his shack at night. His lips moved continuously, as if he were praying. Sometimes he had momentary visions of a village being battered by the wind and of a solitary child sitting by a grave, but they instantly vanished. Tedla the Crazy seemed like a wise elder who pondered important matters related to both heaven and earth. Everyone nodded at him with reverence as they passed by.

After the heavy rains passed, when the sky over the high plains was cleansed of all humidity and at its most intense azure, with only a few stray clouds decorating it like the purest of bows, Tedla would go out in the early morning hours and sit at the base of a solitary agave plant. Listening to the noises of the day as he got ready to face its new challenges, feeling the warmth of the sun on his skin, which at that hour shone light and clear, the old man felt at peace.

One morning a little girl walked up to him. She was small and skinny and had a long braid. Her dark eyes were filled with a golden glow and she peered at him intently, as if trying to learn his secret.

'What's your name?' Tedla asked her.

'Marianna,' she replied instantly, as if she had been waiting for the question so that she could start talking to the old man. 'I'm on my way to school. I have to go all the way to Mai Bela.'

She peered at him closely to see how her words affected him. No one in Edaga Arbi went to school. Sellass had decided that her children needed to learn to read and write, that they could not be uneducated like the poor folk around them. By sending Marianna to school and Gianfranco to nursery school, she was also protecting them from neighbourhood dangers and from feeling lonely. She had dipped into her little pile of savings to pay for the schools and, as a result, lost a number of nights' sleep wondering how much longer she would have to wait before she could buy a house. Luckily, she received tips from Italian clients and brought dinner home to the children.

Despite her mother's rules, Marianna continued to spend too much of her free time outdoors. It was hard for Sellass to focus on her work, thinking of her daughter out wandering around. But Marianna continued to chase after colourful butterflies and explore the village, keeping away the cruel children with both rocks and rage, which gave her a boost of courage.

When the market came to town, she visited all the stalls, from start to finish, getting very excited at anything new. She followed the *beles* vendors, who came from neighbouring villages with their containers full of prickly pear fruit and chattering, petulant monkeys perched on their shoulders. She brought Gianfranco with her and showed him the monkeys and explained – as one of the beles vendors had told her – that those funny animals were their distant brothers.

Sellass beat Marianna each night when she came home, even when the child had spent the day indoors or in the courtyard, impatiently waiting for evening to fall. At that point, Marianna figured it was better to go out and discover new things – butterflies, the market, an enormous puddle that held all the clouds in the sky – and listen to the prickly pear vendors' stories.

Now Marianna stood staring at the old man with the gentle expression; two moths had got caught in his long white beard and his long hair was tangled with blades of grass.

Elsa, who enjoyed telling the children stories, had told them all about the crazy man named Tedla who had lived for years and years on the streets of Asmara and who used to sleep in an open grave at the cemetery. She said that Tedla had been brought by the wind to Asmara when he was a baby, and he had been left all alone to take care of himself. The wind had been a strong and cruel master of his village, screaming with rage during the day and night, causing houses and plants and people to tremble with fear. It destroyed the village where Tedla had lived and scattered the inhabitants across the mountains like so many crazed butterflies. Despite the fact that the wind was capricious and moody and whimsical, it liked the boy who always stood off to one side, watching worldly things with a sense of wonder, so it decided to carry him across the valleys and mountains and leave him in Asmara, where someone would surely take care of him. The wind then erased all Tedla's memories of both his village and his large family, so that he would never feel nostalgia for his lost dear ones. And this is how Tedla came to grow up in darkness, with neither longing nor grief, unaware that he was a child of the wind.

'Are you Tedla, the child of the wind?' Marianna asked in a whisper and with amazement, but then immediately regretted it. Elsa had told her that he had no recollections of the past.

The old man smiled, glad to set eyes on the little girl and hear someone pronounce his name, and nodded.

Marianna sat down next to him for a few minutes. She wanted to show him that she was his friend.

'I like going to school,' she said, carefully smoothing down the dress that her mother had asked an Arab tailor to stitch together quickly. 'One of the teachers is Italian and she likes me, and there are no Eritrean children because they don't go to school.' She looked up at the old man. His lips were moving silently and he was smiling. He seemed happy to have a little friend.

'There are a few Italian girls, a couple of mixed-race girls and lots of Indians,' Marianna continued. 'Everyone thinks I'm Indian. They like me.' She glanced quickly at the old man, who nodded at her to show his agreement.

'I have to go now,' Marianna said, standing up to leave. 'But I'll come back and visit you again.'

And so Marianna came to have yet another friend in Edaga Arbi. She was glad to know Tedla, the child of the wind, and whenever she stopped to talk to him, he would smile at her and his eyes would light up. One day he gave her a beautiful feather that he had saved just for her.

Whenever Marianna heard the voice of the wind blow through town, whenever she saw red clouds of dust rise up angrily from the ground, she would drag an angareb up to the door to block the wind from coming in and hold Gianfranco tightly, so that no one could ever take him away.

20

The owner of the trattoria where Sellass worked was energetic, cheerful and pleasant with everyone. She had come to Africa with her husband some years before the war. Originally from Reggio Emilia, the couple had both worked in a pasta factory that eventually went out of business; with only a little money but a great deal of entrepreneurial spirit, they decided to open a trattoria in Asmara.

Those were the years when people with ideas and the desire to work hard could build a good life for themselves in the Italian colony, even if they arrived with only a little money. People who had experienced poverty in Italy rapidly made their fortunes in Eritrea; the Italian enclave was like a garden of Eden. The business started by the Rubini family became a point of reference for many Italians: Signora Giovanna was a good cook and her dishes had all the flavours and aromas of their homeland. When the brief illusion of an African colony faded, thousands of emigrants returned home, regretting everything they were forced to leave behind, while others stayed on in the hopes that those sad and uncertain times would pass and they would go back to living in peace.

The Rubini family stayed on, but then the husband died of typhoid fever and Signora Giovanna had to handle everything on her own. This was a time when there was a shortage of many of the basic foodstuffs and not many customers; the general mood of having lost the war was oppressive.

But times improved, Signora Giovanna worked hard, and the trattoria went back to being a popular spot.

When Sellass came looking for a job and said she knew how to cook, Giovanna hired her immediately: she was pretty, she had pleasant manners and she even spoke some Italian.

Giovanna was an outgoing woman and liked to talk as well as listen. She was curious but not intrusive. She would have liked to learn more about Sellass and her past — actually, she was very curious — but she detected that Sellass did not want to talk about herself. All she said was that she came from Massawa and that she had two children. Giovanna decided to try her out and was relieved to discover that Sellass was a hard worker. She helped in the kitchen and also served tables; she was tidy and clean; the clients liked her and left her tips. Occasionally men stared at her, but she let them know that she was not interested in talking to anyone about anything other than work. In the evenings, after tidying up the kitchen, she would wrap up some leftovers in a white napkin that the Signora had given her and take them home. There was usually a little bit of everything and the children would open the bundle with excitement, as if it were a box of magic. As soon as Sellass walked in, Marianna and Gianfranco ran up to her, kissed her dress repeatedly, and waited anxiously for her to put the food down on the table. Sellass had to wake up before dawn because the trattoria was a long way from Edaga Arbi and there was always much to do. While she worked, she did her best to ignore the suffering in her heart, which was with her from the moment she opened her eyes in the morning and weighed so heavily that sometimes it left her short of breath.

She worried about the children, about leaving them on their own for so long, and about all the dangers that existed in the village, where they were not looked upon kindly. She often thought about Marianna, how she constantly went out exploring, looking for excitement in order to escape that devastating solitude, and about Gianfranco, how he sat in the corner, sucking his thumb, his eyes staring emptily ahead. Yet somehow she always managed to find an excuse to beat her daughter.

After talking to the priest – every month she gave him a gift of some sugar or coffee, like all the Eritrean women did – she decided to send Gianfranco to a nursery school run by the nuns and Marianna to a school near Mai Bela. She wanted to give them an education, but this did not erase the bitterness at having to spend money on school, and it cost almost her whole salary. She would simply have to put off buying a house for a little longer.

One of her regular clients at the trattoria was a handsome, though no longer young, gentleman who left her generous tips and furtively caressed her hand when she placed a plate down in front of him. He was always alone and sometimes stayed until closing time, drinking and smoking.

One night, after leaving, Sellass heard someone call her name. It was him. He had waited for her and invited her to join him in his automobile.

Sellass walked off swiftly, covering her face with her futah. The gentleman followed her for some distance until they got to the grain market, when he stopped his car and got out. The scent of spices still lingered in the air and the darkness was filled with the song of crickets. Sellass was scared. The man's swift footsteps echoed across the cobblestones in the still night, as if they were treading on her, trampling her body. He caught up to her quickly, he was tall and strong, she felt his hands grab her shoulders. For a moment she thought of Carlo, that night in Massawa, the quick heartbeat in her chest; but she had not been afraid back then, she had heard the distant splashing of waves and smelt the sea, and then he had kissed her.

'I don't want to hurt you,' the man said gently. 'I only want to drive you home.'

Sellass felt as though she had turned to stone. She stared straight ahead of her and into the darkness.

'You're very beautiful, Sellass,' the man said, his hands squeezing her shoulders even more firmly. Sellass thought back to Carlo and felt a languor run through her body, just like it had all those years ago. She let the man run his hands slowly down her body but then stepped back.

'Leave me alone,' she said. 'Let me go.'

'I know you've already slept with an Italian and that you have two children. I know everything about you.'

Again, Sellass tried to tell him to leave.

'Let's go into the car. I'll give you money so you can buy things for your children.'

'Go away,' Sellass said, the words catching in her throat. 'I don't want anything from you, let me go.'

'Lots of women with mulatto children sleep with men, especially white men. I can help you...'

Sellass felt her fortitude fading. He managed to get her into the car, lifted her dress, but when Sellass smelt his bad breath, she pushed him away, scratched him, opened the car door and clambered out. Trembling with anger and filled with hatred for everything and everyone, she felt her strength return to her with a force she had never known before.

Just then, a group of Indian teenagers passed by. Sellass caught up to them and stayed close until she heard the car drive off.

When she got home, it was very late. The children had fallen asleep on the ground, waiting for her.

Sellass threw herself down on the bed without even taking off her futah. She could still feel the man's hands on her breasts and was reminded of moments from her final night with Carlo.

The painful memory of his face, which she had tried so terribly hard to erase from her mind, came back to her as clearly as if they had just left each other.

The following day Sellass was restless and in a bad mood. Giovanna realised that something was wrong but Sellass would not tell her what was bothering her. She wished she could throw herself down on the ground the way the women in her village used to do when they felt desperate, the way her aunt Alefesc did when the demon Zar came and possessed her; she wished she could scream and shout and swear until the day she died; she wished she could become one of those shades that walked across the water at night towards Mariam: freed of all their earthly burdens, they had left behind the world and its suffering, and were the ethereal ambassadors of a kingdom of peace. Mariam, the children of Massawa who used to run to her, the waves that crashed against the rocks by the lighthouse – all were a distant dream, something she must have invented in a moment of peace, or part of a past life that had already vanished to some far corner of the world.

While recalling Mariam's shells, imagining them in the shape of a flower on the warm cobblestones, Sellass carelessly spilt a pan of hot oil, in which she was frying potatoes, onto her arm and chest. She screamed with all her might at the terrible pain. Giovanna rushed her to the hospital where she was medicated; she had been burnt badly, they said, and would have to return for treatment.

Sellass never went back to Giovanna's trattoria. The mere thought of the place made her sick to her stomach. She kept saying to herself, almost obsessively, that she would not serve the whites, but she saw no other possibility for work. Those were terrible days in their sad little home. There were no more dinners of leftovers from the trattoria. They had to get by on a little injera or borgutta or a cup of chai. Sellass could not hide her foul mood, and the children were sad and taciturn.

The only words Sellass ever uttered – over and over, while looking at the children and always in a whisper – were the question her children would never forget: 'How could he…?'

The rainy season had ended, the nights were cold and the children tried to stay warm by snuggling together. The only blanket that Sellass had bought, used, was not enough to keep them warm, and cold air blew in through the holes in the ceiling.

So Sellass went to see the priest and, with his help, found a job working for an Italian family.

Defeated and humiliated, her only hope to one day be able to buy a house, Sellass went and introduced herself to Signora Giustina, who was looking for a young, honest Eritrean woman capable of doing all types of household work.

21

Giustina Prandi was a handsome lady: tall, imposing, with strong features and large blue eyes. Provincial and lacking in imagination, Giustina was principally concerned with maintaining a level of comfort in her home to which she had grown accustomed.

She woke at midday, in time to make sure that lunch was being properly prepared. In the afternoon she dedicated a few minutes to her daughters, who were either busy playing or studying, then she had tea with her friends, and in the evening she went to the Italian social club to play canasta and catch up on all the latest gossip. There were visits to the hairdresser, the seamstress, shopping in town, and time set aside for overseeing the household accounts; Giustina spent a great deal of energy and time on this last activity, making sure the numbers tallied up perfectly.

Her husband was a good and decent man, a careful administrator of the buildings he owned, unwilling to engage in any kind of controversy. At home he spoke little and, to avoid all fuss, he allowed his wife to be the undisputed head of household.

During the little time they spent together, he listened to her absentmindedly, thinking his own thoughts, which had absolutely nothing to do with his wife's comments, counting down the minutes until he could reach his favourite object: his armchair, far from the dining table. He was grateful that destiny had given them two daughters who were quiet, subdued, and studious; they seemed to have been created expressly not to disturb the happy monotony of his life. Every so often he allowed himself an uncompromising dalliance – with a married woman or a willing girl – just to prove to himself that he was still in the vigour of youth. Giustina, although a perfectly attractive lady, appealed to him no more than any piece of household furniture – with the exception of his armchair – and their nights together were founded on rest and repose. Giustina was perfectly content with this arrangement; she had never truly desired a man, not even her husband, and had only married because it was the right thing to do.

Their home, a solid old house in the centre of Asmara, mirrored its inhabitants perfectly. There were heavy dark curtains to keep out the bright sun, stately furnishings in highly polished dark wood, large lacquered paintings of shady landscapes – the works of unknown and talentless painters – and a piano, which the daughters plunked away at with absolutely no ear for music. There were photographs everywhere, testimonials to weddings, baptisms and first communions, as well as numerous busts of grandfathers and great-grandfathers. There were elephant tusks, porcelain ballet slippers, assorted chinoiserie, and a wall clock from which appeared, at fifteen-minute intervals, a chirping cuckoo to remind them of the inexorable passing of time.

The peace of the household was brutally shaken when Maria, the elderly Eritrean woman who had served the Prandi family for years, putting up with the domineering and whimsical manners of the lady of the house, announced that at month's end she would be returning to her village, having reached an age where she felt she could no longer work. Apparently, on that historic occasion even the cuckoo lowered its voice. Giustina, wide-eyed with disbelief and a hand on her heart, accused Maria of terrible ingratitude: old age was just an excuse.

Maria listened calmly while her mistress made her final scene, looked at her as if she were merely one of the many knick-knacks she had dusted over the years, embraced the children, walked through the kitchen to check on a simmering pot of boiled beef, and, taking only as long as she needed, gathered her few belongings from her room in the courtyard and left the house forever. She knew there would be no severance pay and she had received her wages two days earlier. The little money she had managed to save up would go to her children and grandchildren to pay for the expenses related to her final years. In the village where she would await death, she would be surrounded by the many children of her large family, and the joy and wonder of the young would bring warmth to her heart.

Immediately following Maria's unexpected departure, Giustina ordered the Eritrean boy who tended their garden to keep an eye on the boiled beef and, after touching up her makeup so as not to appear as upset as she truly was, went to a friend's house to announce the bad news and get help finding, as quickly as possible, a capable replacement.

Giustina spent several days in a disagreeable mood, which not only had a negative effect on the smooth functioning of the household, but also caused her to lose all her games of canasta, which had simply never happened before. Her husband made every effort to be at home as little as possible during that period, and the girls continued to play and study, only occasionally mentioning Maria.

Giustina interviewed many Eritrean women recommended to her by friends and acquaintances, but none of them were good enough; it was not easy to find a substitute for a woman like Maria, who knew how to do everything and also had a spirit of initiative.

And then, one morning, as if sent from heaven — in this case, taking the form of the priest from the Coptic church — Sellass appeared.

Initially Giustina felt a twinge of hostility towards the young woman who stood before her. She seemed too proud, as if entitled to something.

Giustina looked her up and down for a few minutes and then asked her some questions. When she learnt that Sellass had worked in Signora Rubini's trattoria, she examined her even more closely. She was attractive and looked clean; if she knew how to do all the chores and cook, she could be the right person to take Maria's place.

Giustina was momentarily perplexed when Sellass told her that she preferred not to sleep in their house but in her own home, in Edaga Arbi.

'You don't have children, do you?' Giustina asked with alarm.

Sellass looked down at her bare feet, recalling how often Carlo had urged her to wear sandals.

'One,' she lied. 'I have a son.'

Giustina sighed and hesitated for a moment before making her decision.

'Fine,' she said. 'You can sleep in your own home. But before you leave at night, you must tidy up perfectly. And you must be here very early in the morning. I demand punctuality and cleanliness,' she said, staring at the young woman, whose expression had not changed. 'Never bring your boy here,' she added. 'Not for any reason whatsoever. And no absences will be tolerated.'

Sellass looked around her, taking in the heavy curtains that darkened the sitting room, the paintings on the wall, and the various knick-knacks, all of which were covered in a thin veil of dust.

'I'll be here tomorrow morning,' she said softly and took her leave.

22

Every morning before sunrise, Sellass made her way quickly down the long road that separated the village of Edaga Arbi from the centre of Asmara.

The air was cold, the sky clear, the houses with their lowered shutters seemed to be fast asleep. The silence was interrupted only by the tolling of the large clock tower, which could be heard across the city.

It did not take long for Sellass to settle in and capably handle all the chores in the Prandi household. Zegai, meanwhile, took care of the garden, the dogs and small maintenance jobs.

Sellass liked the two girls, especially Carla; whenever she spoke the girl's name, she felt an inexplicable flutter of happiness, which then left her feeling empty, forcing her to bury both her memories and her pain.

Sellass did not understand why she felt compelled to beat her daughter for the slightest stupidity and yet shower Carla with affection, when both of them, in different ways, reminded her of Carlo.

Signora Giustina was very demanding and high-strung; something was always wrong. The worst moment of the day, for Sellass, was in the evening, when the food vendors passed by. Giustina would tell Sellass to call for them and then she herself came down, keeping the vendors outside the gate, so that she could check their prices.

The barefoot and malnourished elderly men and women, exhausted from their long trek into the city from the countryside to sell their goods, tried to turn down the Signora's paltry offers, but Giustina always won out, concluding the negotiations by ordering Sellass to go and retrieve the merchandise, hand the vendors the amount she herself had decided upon, and close the gate firmly in their faces.

The poor merchants walked off muttering and swearing. In moments like that, Sellass hated Giustina, and she had to bite her tongue not to swear at her. It was important to Eritreans, at the conclusion of all negotiations, to receive a blessing from the vendor; this was why they always tried to meet them halfway. As a result, whenever Sellass saw the merchants walk off mumbling that God would punish the unjust, she, unable to run out and beg their forgiveness, felt impending misfortune. Despite her air of detachment, Sellass was deeply connected to the beliefs of her people and was afraid of divine punishment.

While Signora Giustina made her way back indoors, pleased at having saved money on her purchases of chickens and vegetables, Sellass would go get a large knife from the kitchen, grab the hen, call Zegai to hold it still, and then, with all her strength, slit its throat. She would then throw the headless chicken down on the ground and watch as it hopped from one end of the courtyard to the other, as if trying not to let life escape through its stump. The head, glassy-eyed and immobile, lay on the ground, accepting of death. After the body of the chicken gave its final shudder, retreating into its bloodied feathers, Sellass instructed Zegai to clean the courtyard while she sat down on the ground to pluck the bird, softly and bitterly counting its feathers.

Sellass had asked Signor Prandi to administer her salary. Every month she received what she needed to pay for school and a few other things and then the gentleman wrote down the remainder on a sheet of paper. Despite earning little, Sellass still hoped to save up enough – together with the money from Carlo that she kept buried underground with the two pearls – for her own house.

Sellass and her children experienced great hardship in Edaga Arbi. Even Zubuc had lost his sheen; his thirsty leaves fluttered sadly through the air before falling into a corner and shrivelling up.

Elsa had not been seen in a long time. A stray dog now sat licking its wounds in the place where she once cooked injera.

Now that Sellass no longer brought home dinner, which had created something of a festive moment each evening, the children knew that they would have to make do with the meal they received at school.

Gianfranco spent a lot of time sitting on the ground, sucking his thumb and biting his nails, or using the pebbles he carried around in his pocket to build towers and then knock them down. He had spoken only once in the past year, to say 'I don't want to go to the nuns' school'. Sellass had asked him some questions but he had not answered her, so she sighed and left him alone in his silence. Although Marianna was slightly jealous of her brother because Sellass never hit him, only her, she would never let anyone mistreat him. Gianfranco seemed to exist in another dimension; he was like one of those angels, Marianna thought, that flew through the sky leaving a trail of colours behind them. Sometimes when she looked into his large sad eyes, she felt a sharp pain in her chest.

None of them had made any friends in Edaga Arbi. Sellass did not stop to talk to anyone and only knew the woman who did her hair every three weeks: unravelling and then re-braiding the many thin plaits.

'Don't go outside,' Sellass said to Marianna every night. 'And don't talk to the people here.'

Marianna nodded in fear. She knew that 'the people here' did not want to talk to them either, but she disobeyed her mother and went out every day, getting as far away as possible from that hostile place.

When she was forced to stayed indoors, in that cold and dark room, without even a single ray of sunshine, she felt overwhelmed with anguish and loneliness.

In fact, when she and Gianfranco had whooping cough, and she had not been able to go outside for many days on end, Marianna had grown deeply melancholic. She had spent hours building up towers of pebbles and then knocking them down with her brother, erasing all thoughts of the outside world, as if it, too, felt crushing grief and had run away somewhere to die.

When night came and their room was illuminated by the weak light of a candle, Marianna brought her ear down to the ground and listened for her mother's returning steps. But when Sellass finally walked through the door, tired and on edge, Marianna's heart started to pound fast. She had even stopped kissing her mother's dress.

Marianna knew that her mother would find a reason to take her anger out on her, so she sought refuge in sleep. It was the fastest way to make sure the daylight would return.

23

Signora Antonella handed Marianna back her notebook and smiled. 'Well done,' she said. 'I'm very pleased with your work.'

The child stared at her teacher, noticing her dark eyes, gentle smile and small crooked teeth.

She wished she could take her teacher's smile and press it between the pages of her book, just like the feather Tedla had given her, or one of Zubuc's golden leaves. Her only wish was for that moment to last forever. She focused on it with great intensity so that it would never die, trying with all her might to tuck away Signora Antonella and her words in some hidden corner of space and time. But the teacher had already moved on to another child, the moment had passed, other words resonated through the sun-filled room.

'Signora Maestra,' Marianna called out.

'Yes?' The teacher walked back to her desk.

'Am I learning to write?'

'Of course you are, Marianna. I even said you're very good at it.'

The child placed her notebook down on her desk and caressed it gently. She was happy. The hours she spent at school were joyful ones; Signora Antonella was the kindest person she had ever met, besides Elsa and Tedla.

She looked around to see her classmates' reaction to what the teacher had said to her. Luckily there were no Eritrean children, she thought to herself. They would've hated her, just like the children in Edaga Arbi or the ones near the market did. There were several Italian girls in the class but Marianna had not been able to make friends with any of them. Once, Elisa, the youngest of them, had lent her a pencil. The Indian girls were friendly: she and Sehila walked part of the way home together, as far as the grain market. Her father's shop, with all its brightly coloured Indian fabrics that Marianna admired, was not far from there.

The other mixed-race girls were all older. One of them, Lina, had a limp. She also had a difficult time learning and speaking, but Signora Antonella was always very patient with her and never berated her. Occasionally, Lina's mother came to pick her up; she was very pretty, dressed and coiffed like the European women. Someone once told Marianna that Lina's mother was a 'lady of pleasure.' When she had asked her mother what that meant, Sellass got angry and slapped her.

Looking at Lina, Marianna felt a dull pain inside. Even though she knew the girl lived in Amba Galliano, in a real house, not like hers in Edaga Arbi, it seemed like she led a sad life. Lina's mother, despite her large eyes outlined in kohl, conveyed the same anguish that her mother did with her long silences and dark, remote stare.

Now and then, Marianna tried to approach Lina and talk to her, but they only exchanged a few timid smiles and whispered salutations at the school gates. Marianna spent a lot of time worrying about how much her school cost her mother; she felt guilty, despite knowing that Sellass wanted her children to be educated. Every night she showed her mother her notebook with her good grades, explaining that high marks were written in blue and low ones in red, so that Sellass could tell the difference, even though she did not know how to read.

Thursday was their free day and Marianna spent it outdoors, exploring, far from Edaga Arbi.

It was on one of her adventures that she met Suor Ernesta. When she saw the nun from afar, in her long black habit, Marianna ran up to her and knelt down and kissed the hem, recalling having seen her mother and others kiss the robes of Coptic priests.

The nun, who was tall, skinny and wore thick eyeglasses, looked down in amazement at the child and told her to stand up.

'I go to Signora Antonella's school, near Mai Bela. Today is our free day,' Marianna told her with a hint of pride.

'You go to Signora Antonella's school?' the nun asked with surprise. 'What kind of work does your mother do?'

'My mother works for an Italian family.'

The nun was quiet for a moment. 'Is your mother a servant? How can she afford to send you to private school? Does she have money to throw away?'

Marianna felt her sense of guilt intensify. She looked down at the ground.

'You should come to our school,' the nun said, taking off her glasses and wiping the lenses with a handkerchief. 'It doesn't cost anything.'

'Do you teach children how to read and write?' Marianna asked in amazement.

'Of course we do,' the nun said. 'We teach children to write just like Signora Antonella does. People like your mother should bring their children to us. Tell her to come and talk to me in Acria.'

'My mother can only come very, very early in the morning,' Marianna said.

'Tell her that she'll even find me there at dawn.'

Marianna watched the nun as she put her glasses back on. She did not resemble Signora Antonella and there was something shifty in her small eyes.

'My brother goes to nursery school with the nuns,' Marianna said to mollify her.

Suor Ernesta looked carefully at Marianna: she was a pretty child, she had dimpled cheeks, her braid was greased with Abyssinian butter, and she was wearing cardboard shoes tied with pieces of twine.

'Don't go wandering about,' she said to her sternly. 'Or you'll come to a bad end too.'

Marianna knelt down again to kiss the hem of the nun's habit but the nun held out the crucifix fastened to her belt. The child hesitated for a moment and then brought her lips to the cold metal.

She watched the nun walk off. She looked like a bird that had been forced to walk instead of fly, her big dark wings fluttering slightly in the breeze as she dragged them behind her.

Marianna was excited. Her mother would be happy when she told her about the nun and the free school; this way she would be able to save her earnings for the house. And yet the thought of leaving Signora Antonella, the sun-filled room and her classmates distressed Marianna. The nun had not smiled the way Signora Antonella did, and her beady eyes had made Marianna feel uncomfortable.

That evening, Sellass got home later than usual. Gianfranco was already asleep, thumb in mouth, while Marianna sat on the ground, counting her thoughts. This was her new hobby, a recent invention: whenever she felt terribly lonely, she counted the thoughts that filled her head. The goal was to store them away in a hidden cellar of her mind from which they'd never be able to escape, and only take them out one at a time to share with Elsa.

Because Elsa understood even the oddest things. If, for example, Marianna wanted to tell her about thought number three – that she suspected that a hidden treasure lay at the bottom of the lake in Acria, which undoubtedly held many secrets in its deep reddish waters – Elsa would understand, and together they would go to the lake to look for it.

'Twelve,' Marianna said quietly as her mother walked in, getting to her feet and writing down the number in a corner of her notebook. While greeting Sellass, she gauged her mother's mood. The woman said something that the child didn't understand, then pulled a small bottle out of her dress and set it on the table.

'Some broth,' Sellass said. 'Drink it.'

When Marianna picked up the small bottle, its warmth filled her with joy. Sellass had held it close to her chest on her long journey home to keep it safe. The child took a sip; there was only a little bit.

She left the remainder for Gianfranco. He would probably wake up during the night from the cold, or to bite off a fingernail, which he would then leave in the bed.

'I met a nun today,' Marianna began. 'She lives in Acria. She told me that their school is free. She wants to talk to you.'

Sellass removed her futah, then looked at Marianna. 'You stupid girl,' she said quietly, clenching her lips. 'Always going out, wandering around, believing whatever people say. I pay for you to go to school, but you'll end up becoming a good-for-nothing all the same…'

Marianna backed up towards the wall, as she always did when she was afraid, trying to recall a thought, one that she had just finished counting, one with lots of colours, to distract her. But she couldn't think of any. Her mother stood staring at her as if she hated her.

'But their school is free,' the child muttered softly. 'And you'll be able to save up for a house. She really was a nun, the kind with the black dress and a cross.'

Sellass sat down heavily on her bed. Marianna realised that her mother wouldn't beat her tonight, even though she was in a bad mood. So Marianna took off her cardboard shoes and crawled under the blanket next to Gianfranco. It felt so good to feel the warmth of his body. She pulled the blanket up over her head and fell asleep. All the thoughts that she had counted up and stored away came to her in her dreams, in unison. From the buried treasure that rose up out of the lake of Acria – shiny gold and pearls, splendid necklaces like the ones she had seen in the centre of town, carpets woven with scenes from fables – came a length of barbed wire that led towards and past the images of her other thoughts – the flamingos, Elsa's flowers, the courtyard of the insane asylum in Amba Galliano – and on to Edaga Arbi, where it pierced Zubuc's heart. The plant trembled, his leaves transformed into small birds, and flew away. Zubuc pulled his branches in close to his trunk and blood began to gush from his hidden heart – which Marianna could not see but heard beating – and turned into the reddish hues of the lake of Acria, where Marianna sank into the mud and struggled to breathe.

She passed a troubled night. When she awoke before dawn, she decided to get up and go outside.

She couldn't stand the thought of remaining there, in that bed, in that room of nightmares, listening to her mother breathe. Sellass would never fully understand how much Marianna loved her and wanted to see her happy.

The thought of her mother weighed like a stone on Marianna's heart. Never again, she told herself, would she count her mother's steps homeward. It was better to count her own thoughts and then put them away somewhere safe, for they would never betray her.

With her heart beating fast, she got dressed and made her way to the door, shoes in hand. Before opening it, she stood still for a moment to make sure that Sellass had not heard her. All she could hear was her own heartbeat and Sellass and Gianfranco's breathing.

The slow creak of the door as it opened was torturous, as if all of Edaga Arbi had been shaken by thunder. She stood immobile for another few seconds, holding her breath, again afraid that Sellass would wake up. Then she closed the door behind her and walked towards the gate.

When she passed Zubuc, she caressed his leaves, as always, both out of affection for the plant and for good luck. It was one of the many rituals she had created for herself and could not refrain from doing. Despite being eager to leave, it felt like she had not petted him enough, so she went back, twice, three times. She needed to be sure that Zubuc's heart wasn't wounded. It wasn't, but his leaves were weak and tired and looked like they might drop merely with a glance. Marianna vowed to find a remedy, so Zubuc could regain his former splendour. The beles vendors had mentioned a sorceress who lived near Devil's Canyon capable of healing all kinds of ills. To win her friendship, you had to bring her a gift.

With great effort, Marianna pushed away the boulder that kept the rusty tin gate closed. Finally, she was outside.

She took a deep breath of relief and dried her sweaty palms on her dress. The black night sky was fading; a glow lay on the horizon. Marianna felt both joy and freedom. Gone was the feeling of oppression she had experienced upon waking.

Then she noticed a distant movement in the rosy dawn light.

Approaching slowly, the way a dream brings a fairy-tale vision into focus, was a caravan of camels.

Marianna remembered one of the beles vendors telling her about the men from the low plains, how they spent the night in the village of Acria on their way to sell their goods at the market.

Tall, slender men wearing elaborate jackets and loose white trousers, tight at the ankle, walked one behind the other, each with the same light step. They sang softly in Arabic as they marched.

The camels followed with the same rhythm, like vessels on a choppy sea.

The men got closer and closer. Marianna was perspiring with emotion, she had never seen such beautiful men, such rich clothes.

The last stars vanished into the light sky; the village and red earth were now visible.

Marianna felt hypnotised by the vision. She could not move. The men came even closer, she could see their handsome and proud faces, their large dark eyes, the golden stitching on their clothes. They paraded past her silently, one after the other, as if connected by an invisible thread.

Meanwhile, the men stared back at her. Marianna felt the reciprocity in their gaze, as if they wanted to communicate to her the disquieting vision that lay before them: a child standing perfectly still, in awe, wearing her long hair loose and a lightweight dress, which surely did little to protect her from the cold. For them, she was the final invention of the night as it abandoned the village: she was a dream, forgotten with the arrival of dawn. When the camels passed in front of her, Marianna tried to imagine the treasures they carried, which would be sold at the market: precious woven fabrics, rare seashells, necklaces, ankle bracelets, and endless blocks of shiny salt, just like the beles vendors had told her.

While she watched them walk away, they turned around one last time to look at her. And then the caravan was gone. She heard noises coming from the village.

Marianna hurried back into the courtyard, quietly closed the gate behind her, ran quickly over to kiss and caress Zubuc, sharing her joy with the bush, and slipped back into bed only a moment before her mother woke up.

She would see them again, she told herself. There would be other dawns when she would venture out beyond the gate to meet her silent new friends.

24

Although Keren was not that far from Asmara, the bus ride to get there was long. The road was winding and the bus trundled along, old and tired. It was crowded with women carrying large overflowing zembil; chickens whose feet had been tied; dirty, sleepy children; men and their heavy sacks of dried grains. Strong odours, from both spices and humans, hung heavily in the heat.

Sellass and Marianna sat at the back of the bus.

Someone had told Sellass about a boarding school specifically for mixed-race girls, in Keren, managed by nuns.

It was quiet there, they said, and the nuns did not want to be paid. In exchange, the girls had to do small odd jobs around the convent.

Sellass was fed up with Marianna spending her afternoons outside, wandering around, so boarding school seemed like a good solution, at least for a period. They even said that Keren was pretty and that the air was good.

When they got off the bus, a bit before midday, the malaise that had filled Marianna for the duration of the trip grew even more acute. She stopped short in the main square, like a goat that refuses to follow its owner after realising it is being led to slaughter.

'Come,' Sellass said, grabbing her hand.

Marianna looked around. The houses were low and white, there were many flowering shrubs and the intense scent of *zaitun* fruit filled the air. Men in long white djellaba and embroidered caps sat on straw mats crafting articles of gold and silver.

The women of the low plains wore shiny rings in their noses, large dangly earrings and moved harmoniously, tightly bound in bright fabrics. Colourful birds flew between the branches, singing as if inebriated with light and life.

The air felt pleasantly warm on her skin.

It occurred to Marianna that, if she were there for any other reason, she would have considered the vibrant little city very pretty.

'I can go to school at the convent in Acria,' she said to her mother, refusing to hold her hand. 'It doesn't cost anything there either. I don't want to go to boarding school.'

The words came rushing out of her in one breath as if it had taken her great courage to say them.

'Hush,' Sellass said to her. 'I know what needs to be done. I'm doing this to protect you.'

The 'boarding school' run by the nuns was a large, white building with a garden in front and a large piece of land behind, where they grew tobacco.

Mother and daughter were greeted by a young nun and shown into the foyer. Sellass explained why they were there, and was told by the woman to wait, that she would go speak to the Mother Superior on their behalf. The young sister was gone for quite a while and returned with a short, stocky nun with hairy moles on her plump face.

'I'm sorry,' the older woman said, looking at Sellass and Marianna. 'But we don't have room for another child. There are so many mulatto girls now...'

Sellass felt uncomfortable, as if the nun were judging her for bringing yet another mixed-race child into the world. Marianna looked at the nun kindly, pleased to hear there was no room for her.

'You really can't do anything?' Sellass said quietly.

'No, nothing,' the nun replied, patting Marianna's face with her fat hand and staring at her through semi-shut eyes. Sellass felt even more ill at ease and regretted having asked a second time.

The Mother Superior sighed and looked at the watch attached to her belt. 'You should have enquired before coming. You would have saved yourself a journey.' She looked at Marianna again. 'Try asking the nuns in Asmara; send her to school there.' She nodded farewell and walked off.

The younger nun felt awkward, and wished she could help.

'Allow me to show you our girls,' she said, inviting Sellass and Marianna to follow her.

They walked down a long, shadowy hall and exited the back of the building. Little girls, only a few years old, all dressed in blue, were patting down mounds of earth and moistening them with pails of water they could barely lift.

'They're planting seedlings for tobacco plants,' the nun said. 'They're our little gardeners.'

Marianna felt deeply pained, and it suddenly became hard to breathe. She glanced at her mother's face, but she remained expressionless.

The little girls stopped their work. They stood very still, none of them moved or spoke. No taller than the tobacco plants themselves, they seemed to be part of the plantation.

'Say hello,' the nun said.

Their mouths moved but no sound came out. Their faces were like dark flowers on spindly stalks.

'Many of the girls have no mothers. They were abandoned,' the nun said.

Marianna realised that she could never stay there. There was more sadness in that boarding school than in all of Edaga Arbi. Despite the fact that the air was breezy and bright and that they were surrounded by singing birds and colourful plants, this was a place of oppression; the girls in blue had ended up there by mistake. It was impossible to look at them without feeling sick with grief.

The nun noticed their discomfort. 'The girls are shy, they're not used to seeing people,' she said. 'We dedicate our lives to them, we're one big family.'

'Thank you,' Sellass said when they reached the front gate again, and knelt down to kiss the nun's crucifix. Then she took Marianna by the hand and they walked back towards the bus stop in the main square.

A crippled woman followed them for a bit, muttering a prayer.

'Were you hoping to leave your daughter there?' the woman asked Sellass, touching her dress humbly. The old woman's eyes reminded Sellass of Mariam.

'What do you want from me?' she asked, trying to remain collected.

'I saw you come out of that place,' the crippled woman said. 'You did well not to leave your daughter there. They treat the children like servants and punish them harshly, even if they wet their beds. I know all about it because my granddaughter works there as a maid.'

Marianna squeezed her mother's hand. Sellass took a small pouch from her dress, removed a coin, handed it to the woman and strode off.

'May God bless you,' the mendicant said.

Marianna turned around to look at her, wishing she knew exactly how they punished the children. For the first time, she was happy to return to Edaga Arbi. She hoped her mother would stop and admire the precious necklaces that the silversmiths had on display, or look at the woven straw baskets that were being loudly offered for sale by women and children, but Sellass walked right past them, wondering if they would have to wait long for a bus back to Asmara.

They were surrounded by beggars, cripples, lepers, and women with sick children strapped to their backs. But there were also pretty girls, water-carriers who sang as they walked, and shepherds with herds of sheep. There was even an elderly woman cooking injera on her mogogo. Marianna thought sadly of Elsa.

'Elsa doesn't come to town anymore to make injera,' she said to her mother.

'Elsa is old,' Sellass said, squeezing her daughter's hand.

Marianna was relieved that her mother was not riled by the fact that there was no room for her at the school: she did not seem to be angry, she had even squeezed her hand. Marianna would have liked to ask if she could go to school with the nuns in Asmara, but she did not dare. Then it occurred to Marianna that it must be hard for Sellass to have mixed-race children, or 'bastards,' as Mebrat had called them.

Although Elsa had told her that mixed-race children had turned out better than the rest, no one that Marianna knew seemed to think so. The main thing now was to get back to Asmara; and one day, she would go looking for Elsa.

They had to wait for an hour in the square for the bus to arrive from Agordat.

Sellass had been given a day off by Signor Prandi; it was a relatively easy period for Sellass as Signora Giustina was in Italy, visiting relatives. Signor Prandi never criticised her, he was not demanding and he was out of the house much of the time. Life without Signora Giustina around was very different.

A fruit vendor approached Sellass and Marianna as they sat waiting for the bus.

He was a child, not much taller than Marianna, he might have had rickets, the whites of his large eyes were yellow. He rested his zembil full of zaitun on the ground. The smell was so intense that Marianna breathed it in deeply, closing her eyes. The boy smiled, picked up one of the fruits and held it up to her face.

'How much?' Sellass asked, pulling out her pouch again.

She bought two zaitun, gave one to Marianna and put away the other for Gianfranco.

Marianna admired the fruit and then offered some to her mother.

'No,' Sellass said, looking off into the distance. 'I don't want any.'

Marianna was deeply moved. She realised that her mother had bought her the fruit as a token of affection. Gently she rubbed it across her face and neck so that the perfume of Keren would stay with her, then she broke off a piece and hid it in her pocket for Zubuc. She would bury it in the earth next to him so the plant would benefit from the fruit's rich flavour and aroma. Maybe one day a zaitun tree would grow in the courtyard of their house in Edaga Arbi.

The child with the yellow eyes returned to Marianna a little while later. Perched on his arm was a falcon with a wounded wing. Marianna was amazed at just how large the bird was; she had only seen them up in the clouds, tiny dark creatures in the sky. The boy smiled at her, proud of having impressed Marianna, and she was grateful to him. Other Eritrean children were always cruel to her: she could never talk to them and she had to run through the village to avoid them. Whenever Marianna and Sellass walked past their shacks, the children threw rocks at them and shouted 'Pro-Italia!' The two of them would walk swiftly past without turning around, with Marianna constantly fearing that one of the rocks would strike Sellass and wound her, but her mother never showed any emotion, and expected her daughter to do the same. They crossed the village like shadows moving across the flame-coloured earth. Now and then a pebble would strike Marianna's dress, but gradually the children's taunting faded away.

When the bus pulled into the square, a small crowd formed in front of the door.

25

With great effort, the bus climbed the road towards the high plains. Marianna looked out the window, fascinated by the landscape: the boulders that looked like sleeping giants, the monkeys that peered with curiosity at the passing bus, the foamy white blanket of clouds that formed along the sheer precipices of the road, as if they had come down from the high plains to nestle at night in the deep gullies.

Sellass sat with her eyes closed and hands crossed across her belly. She had not moved once since the bus left Keren.

The landscape blurred before Marianna's sleepy eyes. The euphorbias reached their long prickly arms high up into the sky, tore it into small blue pieces and made bits of it flutter through the air, striving to regain the vast unity it had lost.

The large red sun, now without a sky, tumbled down the cliffs, stopping to rest briefly first on one then another cloud, always heading earthwards, gradually disappearing into the abyss. One ray got stuck on the euphorbias and was transformed into a twisted shiny tree; Marianna saw the falcon with the broken wing perching on one of its branches. The light from the tree was so bright it lit up the field of slender tobacco plants, waving in the wind, bending first this way and then that. The plants themselves resembled the little girls from the school in Keren, their dark faces resting on blue stalks; then the nun with the moles on her face came running and cut them all down with a scythe, transforming them into a large bouquet, which the crippled beggar woman grabbed out of her hand.

The beggar hid the severed children-plants under her futah, together with Marianna, who very much wanted to escape but could not move. She, too, had turned into a poor tobacco plant and would never be able to run away because she had lost the use of her legs.

But then Elsa's flowers, the 'Maria Cristinas,' arrived. They rescued her and took her far away, to Elsa's house in the valley below Ghezzabanda.

There, Marianna was transformed back into a little girl. She climbed the stairs towards her friend's house. The door was ajar. She called Elsa's name several times. A large dark bird on the roof replied, so Marianna opened the door and walked in. The shutters in the room were open; sunlight shone on spiderwebs that hung in a silvery curtain around Elsa's bed from the ceiling. Caught in the spiderwebs were leaves that had blown in on the wind and colourful butterflies and petals from Elsa's white flowers.

Marianna was fascinated by the vast spiderweb curtain; it must have taken thousands of spiders to weave it. She looked around for them but couldn't see a single one. Without touching it, fearful of breaking it, she peered through its delicate pattern towards the bed. There lay Elsa, in a long bright red dress, looking like a small dark doll. Her face was perfectly smooth: all her smile lines had disappeared, and the tattooed cross on her forehead was shiny and black.

The red dress covered her almost entirely. Only her hands were still visible and they lay resting on her belly; her moonstone ring cast a pale and milky light around the room.

'Elsa,' Marianna whispered, knowing the woman would not reply. Her face had never been quite as pretty and at ease, but Marianna was confused as to why her body had become so small.

She wished she could go and embrace her but didn't want to break the spiderweb. Marianna knew that Elsa would never return to Edaga Arbi to cook injera and tell stories.

'Elsa,' she said again, feebly hoping that she was just sleeping.

It then occurred to Marianna that no one would ever be able to take Elsa away from her house or from her flowers; she had often spoken of the long hours she used to spend in the garden, or sitting on the stairs in the evening, watching the sun go down. The spiders would take care of her forever.

The bus halted suddenly for a herd of sheep on the road, the driver swearing at the shepherd. Marianna looked around. The sun was going down. In a few minutes the bus ride would end in the main square of Asmara. Sellass rubbed her eyes and ran her hands across her face.

'Mama,' Marianna said, gently touching her mother's dress. 'Elsa has died. She won't come to Edaga Arbi anymore.'

Sellass looked at her daughter for a moment without saying a thing. 'Yes,' she said softly. 'She died a few days ago.'

'Who told you?' the little girl asked, holding on to her mother's dress.

'Zegai,' she said. 'Everyone knew Elsa.'

Marianna shut her eyes and saw Elsa sitting on the stairs that led to her house. She wouldn't say anything to Gianfranco because he didn't know what death was yet. Nor did she, really. Death meant disappearing, it meant leaving this world. Or maybe it meant hiding away forever. Or else it meant going to a pleasant village outside the walls of the world, a place where everyone eventually went when they were old, and sometimes even when they were young. Because even children died. In any case, death was an abandonment, it meant leaving the living behind without saying anything, it was a kind of betrayal. She wished she could run to Elsa's house, maybe she'd still be lying on her bed. No one would ever manage to bring her to Amba Galliano, to the white people's cemetery.

While Marianna had been thinking these thoughts, the other passengers had all got off the bus. Sellass had waited until the bus was empty.

'Get up,' she said, grabbing her daughter's arm.

Marianna realised that, after that day in Keren, her 'thoughts' now counted thirty-one. There had been the silversmiths, the little boy, the wounded falcon and the zaitun. Although she did not want to transform the little girls or the boarding school into thoughts to be saved, she knew that some thoughts persisted anyway, stubbornly hiding in a nook of her mind, even if she didn't want them. They just sat there in the dark, pretending that nothing had happened, only to suddenly and cruelly reappear.

Mother and daughter walked across town. It was getting dark.

'Mama,' Marianna said, before entering their house. 'I can go to the nuns' school in Acria; even the Mother Superior in Keren said so. It won't cost you anything.'

'How easy everything is for you,' Sellass said with a spark of rage. 'The nuns in Keren didn't want you because you're no good; you're not even good enough to pick tobacco.'

Marianna bit her lip and tried not to cry. She wished she could die, she wanted to leave her mother forever. She resented Elsa for abandoning her without letting her know she would be leaving, without giving her one last chance to share her thoughts.

And then she heard her mother mumbling that familiar phrase.

'How could he...?'

26

The Christmas holidays were approaching, the sky was clear blue and the air was crisp and bright. The windows of the shops in Asmara were filled with nativity figurines, colourful glass orbs, silvery ribbons and boxes of elegantly wrapped candies. Gennaro, the pastry chef on Viale della Regina, was busily preparing his marzipan creations; from his talented hands came lambs, mangers, shepherds playing their zampogna pipes, Magi, as well as beautifully rendered brown chestnuts, which reminded him of his youth in a small Italian town.

Signora Giustina had asked the florist to procure a tall strong tree from the Bet Gherghis forest for them, which would be set up in the living room. She had also purchased a number of bright baubles from the glass shop, as each year some of them fell and broke.

She went to the seamstress every day for fittings of the chiffon dress she would wear to the New Year's Eve celebration at the Circolo Italiano. That soiree was one of the most highly anticipated events of the year: they would ring in the new year with endless bottles of bubbly, orchestra music played by the 'boys,' and dancing. Each of the ladies wanted to be the most elegant, well aware that they would continue to talk about the event for at least a month, commenting on who wore what.

The two young Prandi girls had written their letters to Father Christmas in their careful handwriting, hoping to receive the much-desired bicycles they had seen in a shop in the centre of town.

Signor Prandi did not like being overly involved in the holiday preparations and came up with more excuses than usual for staying out of the house.

Sellass had a great many things to do: take down, clean and rehang the curtains; wash the windows and doors; polish all the silverware.

She was anxious and worried because Signora Giustina had told her that she would not be able to return home on Christmas Eve, that there was simply too much to do, and she couldn't risk not having her servant available to her on that long night.

The lady of the house never asked Sellass about her son, it was as if he did not exist. For her part, Sellass understood that she should never mention him either.

Sellass did not like the white people's Christmas, nor that of her own people, which came two weeks later. She tried not to think about the Christmases she had spent in Massawa, when Carlo brought them sweets and gifts, or how Maurizio came to celebrate with them, telling the children about the elderly man who travelled across the starry skies in his sleigh on that special night.

Although she managed to distance the memories, the suffering remained. On that particular night of celebrations, her children would be lonelier than usual in that desolate house;

all because she was nothing more than a servant, abandoned by a white man.

She tried to put a stop to her thoughts and focus on the floors that needed polishing, the foods that needed to be cooked for lunches and dinners, the linens that needed pressing. Occasionally she wished that the whites would leave her country, but then she was compelled to wonder where her children belonged.

When the little girls came home from school, ran into the kitchen and dipped their pieces of bread into the sauces that she was making, she pretended to get angry with them and shooed them away, but Carla's smile, her affectionate 'Hello, Sellass' brought her a moment of solace. And when she said the child's name in reply, she pronounced it carefully, the same way she had always tried to say 'Carlo.'

One day – Christmas Eve – Zegai approached her as if he had a very important message to deliver. Generally, the boy was afraid of Sellass and her long silences, her gruff manner, and the way she scorned everything and everyone around her. Rarely did he find the courage to speak to her. He carried out her orders with deference also because he was aware that he needed her guidance to accomplish his work well, and when she actually said 'Good work, Zegai' in a kind way, he felt deeply content.

'Sellass,' he said while she was polishing one of the little porcelain ballerinas. 'I need to tell you something.'

Sellass continued to clean the statuette without looking at him. 'Go on,' she said. 'And don't forget to bring the tree inside.'

Zegai looked down at the carpets, with their dark and complex patterns. He spoke softly. 'My cousin has a friend, an important man. He works for the English and went to school and has a lot of money. His name is Marcos, he's not that old, and he has a nice house in Ghezzabanda.'

Sellass put down one ballerina and picked up another.

A few moments passed. She seemed to be ignoring Zegai.

'He…' Zegai cleared his throat and went on. 'He would like to meet you. He sees you walk by his office every evening.'

'Does he need a servant?' Sellass asked and opened the curtains to let in the sunlight.

Zegai felt more awkward than before.

'I do not like serving the white people,' Sellass said. 'But I will not give up this job to serve an Eritrean,' she said, thinking of Edaga Arbi and Mebrat.

'He doesn't want a servant,' Zegai said. 'He has other intentions. He would like to meet you,' he said, glancing back down at the carpet. 'I think he wants to marry you,' he said quickly.

Sellass hastily opened a window, causing the birds that had been sitting on the ledge to fly away in fear.

'It's late,' Sellass said. 'And we have many things to do before evening. Go and take care of the garden, Zegai, and leave me alone.'

Zegai realised that it was pointless to insist and walked out of the room muttering something under his breath, wishing he could fire something back. Unfortunately, any rebellious tendencies he might have had withered under her gaze.

Signora Giustina came and went with packages, the little girls observing her every move, trying to guess what they contained. The night was endless, the wait was long, and they could not be certain that the jolly old man would satisfy all their requests. Sellass was now in a bad mood and stood by her pots and pans, defending them from all intruders.

Later that evening, Sellass set the large table with the family's best china and silverware, while Signora Giustina arranged some cut flowers in the vases.

The large tree stood in a corner on its own, waiting for the children to go to bed before it could be dressed with its ornaments, when it would look, at least for a few days and in all its brilliance, like a pontiff dressed for an extraordinary occasion. But already some of its needles were falling to the ground, hinting at its imminent demise, communicating to the tree that it would never return to the woods; never again would it be able to admire its reflection in the lake. Once the holidays were over, long after the triumphant lighting of the lights, once it had turned into a wretched thing with misshapen limbs, Zegai would leave it outside the front gate. Its final journey would be accompanied by a rain of dry, yellow needles.

Meanwhile, the nativity scene was ready; it was only missing the baby Jesus, who would arrive during the night. A comet shone over the manger. In addition to the usual figurines, there was even a well with real water and three palm trees. Joseph and Mary, looking very lonely, huddled over a cradle, empty except for a bit of straw. Earlier, Shoà, the Prandis' cat, had cautiously reached out a paw and knocked over the entire herd of sheep. Giustina had screamed and Carla had quickly shut the cat in another room.

And then the dinner guests arrived: Signor Prandi's parents; one of his brothers with his wife and child; and a friend of Giustina's – 'the lively spinster' as she was known at the Circolo – who wore a dress that resembled a Christmas tree.

Signora Giustina had given precise instructions to Sellass, knowing full well that it was unnecessary because the girl knew exactly what needed to be done. But the lady of the house was so anxious and excited that she had to direct some of her tension onto someone else. Sellass' indifference and hauteur often put Giustina in a bad mood; more than once the lady had complained to her husband that she could not stand the girl's arrogance any longer, at which point he would remind her of Sellass' positive qualities and just how difficult it would be to find a replacement for her.

That night Sellass worked until late, cleaning the kitchen and preparing for the following day's lunch. Signor and Signora Prandi were busy decorating the tree: every so often a glass ball broke and Giustina would swear, the star gave them trouble, and the highest branch had already lost all its needles.

The cathedral bells rang long and loud, announcing the holy Mass, as if they had waited all year to ring out in a glorious concert that filled the night air with joy. Baby Jesus awaited the faithful in the large-scale nativity scene in the festooned church.

Then silence fell over the city.

The streets were dark and deserted. The only sound that could be heard was the call of a distant night bird.

Sellass lay down on the camp bed in the courtyard room. She did not even take off her clothes; she had to be up again at dawn. She shut her eyes and thought of the children, all on their own, in Edaga Arbi. She thought of how Marianna spent her vacation days wandering around, how Gianfranco sat in the corner, biting his nails. Maybe they would play with pebbles, maybe Marianna would tell her brother one of the fanciful stories she always invented for him. It occurred to Sellass that, as the children of an Italian, this was their Christmas, too. She banished the images that came into her mind, covered her head with her futah and fell asleep. In her dreams she smelled the briny scent of low tide by the salt flats.

27

Marianna spent the afternoon of Christmas Eve rummaging through bins and scouring the streets for empty cigarette packets; from them she extracted the small sheets of silvery paper. Then she gathered some dried branches.

Her Italian classmates had talked at length about Christmas trees, nativity scenes, baby Jesus, and the old man who would bring them presents.

Sellass had left for work that morning before dawn, leaving some injera and scirò that ought to have lasted Marianna and Gianfranco for both the festive days, but the children were hungry and ate everything immediately. Sellass had told them that neither Father Christmas nor baby Jesus existed, that parents were the ones who brought children presents that night but that they lied to their children to make them happy.

'If they really existed,' Sellass had said, 'they would visit all the children.'

Marianna accepted what her mother said and had been briefly tempted to tell her classmates the truth, but then she decided to let them have their illusion. At the same time, she didn't want to forego the celebration entirely and wanted to bring Gianfranco some happiness, so she came home that evening with the pieces of silver foil and dry branches.

'Go get all your pebbles,' she said to Gianfranco. 'We're going to make a beautiful tree, you'll see.'

He looked at her in wonder, then ran to get his pile of pebbles that he kept hidden near Zubuc.

'Zubuc has only one leaf left,' he told her when he returned, breaking his usual silence. 'Two of them have already flown away.'

'We have to cover him with something tonight, because if he loses the last one, he'll die. And he can't die tonight.'

Gianfranco rested the pebbles at Marianna's feet, stuck his thumb in his mouth, and stared at the branches and pieces of paper that his sister had collected. Marianna realised that Gianfranco had great expectations of her; she had not seen him this caught up in one of her projects in a long time and did not want to let him down.

'Help me,' she said, starting to carefully wrap each of the pebbles in the foil. Then she tied the dried branches together with a piece of twine and propped them up against the wall.

Gianfranco tried his best to wrap the pebbles just like his sister did. Marianna told him to be very careful so the silvery paper would not get ruined.

After much effort, the Christmas tree's dry branches were adorned and illuminated by the shiny little bundles; there were even three little chocolates that Signora Antonella had given Marianna.

'Do you like it?' Marianna asked, noticing the expression of awe on her brother's face. Gianfranco stared and stared at the tree, his thumb in his mouth.

'It's beautiful,' he eventually said. 'It looks like a great big light.'

The two children sat side by side, gazing at the tree. Marianna thought about the colourful glass baubles, decorative stars and bright strips of tinsel that she had seen in the shops. She also thought about the real trees that lived in the forest of Bet Gherghis. She was not completely convinced that their tree was that great, but Gianfranco was happy. The pebbles certainly looked special, all wrapped up in silver, and there was nothing shinier than the foil from cigarette packets. Even the room itself seemed pleased with the unexpected gift.

Then Gianfranco fell asleep, his head resting on his sister's shoulder, and Marianna felt a deep sorrow come over her, as if the moment of joy had fizzled out. She thought about her classmates: they had trees, nativity scenes, and gifts; they were spending the evening celebrating with their parents; some of them were even going to Massawa to go swimming. Marianna reflected on the fact that she and Gianfranco had an Italian father and she wondered where he was, who he was spending Christmas with. Maybe he had died, like Elsa, or maybe he lived far away, on the other side of the sea. She had thought a lot about him of late, but she couldn't ask her mother anything because she was afraid of her reaction, intuiting that this was a painful wound that she should never touch. She also knew that Sellass had kept something hidden – buried underground – that he had given her. Marianna had tried to find it on several occasions, hoping to solve the mystery, but was never successful. Suddenly she felt a great desire to sleep. It was very cold and simply lying next to Gianfranco was not enough to get warm. When she was sad, she liked thinking about sleep, about the magical way it quickly erased all the day's troubles and created an enchanted otherworld where all sorts of things could happen: she might encounter Elsa, fly up into the clouds, or see Zubuc with golden leaves; she might find herself in danger and need to escape; giant waves might rise high up into the sky and threaten to come crashing down on her like mountains of water; she might see terrifying chasms filled with lurking shadows, making her heart pound with fear. But daylight always returned. And beyond the walls of their room were so many other things to delight in: the camel drivers, the lake of Acria, butterflies, the large courtyard of the mental hospital in Amba Galliano, where she greeted the mad people through the gate. And then there was Tedla, sitting in his sunny spot, the gardens in the centre of town where colourful flowers grew, and the fountain just outside Ghezzabanda.

With great effort, Marianna picked up Gianfranco and carried him to bed, his thumb never leaving his mouth. She was sorry that he had fallen asleep because she would have liked to tell him a story. She liked inventing fables and he enjoyed listening to them. She told him stories about good wizards who could transform Zubuc into a forest strong enough to pick up their house and carry it up to their friend, the sun, so that he, who had not forgotten how his little friends had waited for him to rise high up in the sky, would fill their home with warm, golden light.

Marianna huddled close to Gianfranco, staring out into the darkness for a long time. Then she heard the cathedral bells ringing: the Christmas concert had travelled all the way to Edaga Arbi. She got up and, even though she was cold, went into the courtyard. She wanted to offer her greetings to Zubuc, cover him with a sheet of paper and bury a little silver pebble in the earth below him; she wanted to listen to the pealing bells and peer into the sky to make sure that an old man with a white beard wasn't driving a cart across the sky on his way to visit other children. She didn't dare touch the last leaf on Zubuc, worried she might hurt him, but she did ask him not to leave them: Zubuc was not allowed to die. It seemed to Marianna that Zubuc noticed the silver pebble because his ailing branches quivered with emotion.

She touched the ground where she had buried the piece of zaitun and promised the bush a little water on Christmas Day.

'If I manage to find the sorceress who lives in Devil's Canyon,' she told him, 'one day soon you may have lots of new leaves.'

She looked up at the dark sky and bright stars. They seemed bigger than usual. She felt a shiver run up her spine. Far off towards Acria, a splendid star with a long tail shone brightly in the sky. It was just like the star in the nativity scene inside the cathedral. She stood staring at it for a long time, afraid that if she moved, it would disappear. But then she hurriedly went and woke up Gianfranco and dragged him out to see the strange star.

The bells stopped ringing and all was silent. It seemed to Marianna that the star was looking down on them with benevolence.

'It's the only one with a tail,' Gianfranco said, comparing it to all the other stars. His voice was thick with sleep. Sometimes her brother didn't understand a thing, Marianna thought, and she led him back to bed. When she came back out to admire it some more, the comet had disappeared.

28

On Christmas Day, Marianna suggested to her brother that they walk to Devil's Canyon, the gully that Ghebre, the beles vendor, had told her about.

She told Gianfranco that it was an enchanted place, that they would see the spirits of the forest there. Marianna didn't want to leave him at home alone on Christmas Day and had to find a way of convincing him to come along.

They walked for a long time, avoiding the Eritrean children whenever possible. Soon they were past the Bet Gherghis forest, where the road began to descend towards Massawa.

A few women were making their way uphill carrying heavy bundles on their back. An old man sat on a rock, talking to himself.

Marianna did not know where Devil's Canyon was exactly and she kept peering over the cliffs along the side of the road for a sign. The air was filled with the shrill sounds of monkeys and birds of prey. They heard a woman singing in a shack nestled between the boulders.

'I'm scared,' Gianfranco said, squeezing Marianna's hand tightly. 'Let's go home.'

'Look,' she said, pointing to a cluster of tukuls built on the edge of a cliff. 'Maybe the sorceress lives there.'

'But what if some children come out?' Gianfranco asked anxiously. Marianna stopped. Her brother was right; maybe it wasn't a good idea to get too close to the houses.

'The sorceress,' she said, 'lives in Devil's Canyon. All sorts of magical spirits live down there with her. There are rivers and lakes, and bushes like Zubuc when he was full of leaves. In fact, I think he might have come from down there. But from up here it's hard to see. We need to call out to her.'

The mountains around them were dotted with prickly pear bushes but they did not run into any of the beles vendors because they were not ripe yet, it was not the season.

'Today isn't a good day for looking for the Devil's Canyon,' Marianna said, glancing around nervously. 'It's a holiday. We'll come back another day.' She had suddenly grown frightened of how alone they were and of the large predatory birds that screamed and swooped down the steep cliffs and into the gullies. It occurred to her that if some cruel man happened by, he could easily push them into one of the dark chasms and there they would remain forever. She started to run, pulling Gianfranco along, who kept stumbling. When they reached Bet Gherghis forest, she felt safe again. They walked to the lake where the trees stood admiring their reflections. When Marianna peered at her own reflection in the water, she was once again overcome with dark feelings: the water had an invisible power that could pull her deep down into its depths, and she could never fight back against it.

She started to run again, but Gianfranco said he was tired. They found a chameleon that had changed colour to blend in with the rock on which it sat. Marianna, thrilled by the discovery, picked it up and wrapped it in a red kerchief that she carried with her. Slowly the chameleon took on a reddish hue.

'See?' Marianna said to her brother to make up for the earlier disappointments. 'It's magic.' They named him Gepir and decided to bring him home. When they got back to Edaga Arbi, the sun was going down. Sellass had already returned.

'Where have you been?' she asked Marianna sternly.

The little girl pinched her brother's arm before replying. 'Not far,' she said, staring straight into her mother's eyes. Gianfranco showed Sellass their Christmas tree. Sellass looked at Marianna and smiled, but more than a smile it was a sneer: the expression she wore in her worst moments.

'It's not ugly,' Marianna said defensively, glancing quickly at her brother, hoping that her mother would realise how happy that simple object had made him.

Sellass did not reply. She was tired and in a bad mood. She looked disparagingly at the dry branches and wrapped pebbles.

'I'm taking you to the convent,' Sellass said. 'There must be someone who can keep you shut in and safe all day. I never know where you are, you always lie to me, and you fill your brother's head with foolish stories.'

Marianna thoughts went to her school, Signora Antonella and the sun-filled classroom. She missed it already.

'In Acria?' Marianna asked softly.

Then Sellass caught sight of the chameleon when it darted out of Marianna's red kerchief.

'We want to keep him,' the little girl said. 'He only eats flies.'

'You did go far away,' Sellass said, grabbing Marianna, shaking and then slapping her. 'I have to find a place where someone can actually teach you a lesson!'

Marianna held the chameleon close to her chest and started to cry.

'A disgrace,' Sellass said gruffly. 'You, too, you're a disgrace.'

29

Suor Ernesta walked across the courtyard, took a large key out of her pocket, and opened the gate. She did not invite Sellass inside, even though it was bitterly cold and dark. The sun had not yet risen. Marianna gripped her mother's dress, almost fearing that her mother would run away.

The nun looked Sellass up and down, then glanced at the child.

'I came about my daughter,' Sellass said softly to the nun.

'You want your child to come to school here?' the nun asked, using big gestures and speaking slowly. Sellass was offended. She understood and could communicate in Italian quite well and did not like being spoken to like that, a manner that many white people used with black people.

'Yes,' she said, going on to choose her words carefully so it was clear what she hoped to obtain. 'My daughter said that you have room for her here.'

'We do,' the nun said, continuing to speak slowly. 'Our school does not cost money, not like the school where she goes now. You work as servant, yes?'

Sellass stared at the nun and her thick eyeglasses, and bit

her lip in frustration. She wanted to walk away. She didn't want anything to do with that idiotic person. But she was a nun, after all. And she'd be able to save money. And her daughter would be kept safe.

'I'll bring her tomorrow morning, on my way to work,' Sellass said.

Suor Ernesta inspected Marianna more closely. She noticed her flimsy cardboard shoes tied with string, her light frock and her skinny arms, mottled by the cold.

'She must always be clean,' the nun said, waiting for Sellass to bow down and kiss her crucifix, but she did not. Marianna, who could tell her mother was annoyed with the nun, made up for her lapse and kissed the hem of the nun's habit.

'Do you go to church?' the nun asked, glowering at Sellass. 'Because you should. You need to ask for forgiveness… for the children.'

Sellass did not reply. She mumbled a barely perceptible farewell, bowed her head, and walked away.

Deeply humiliated, Sellass squeezed Marianna's hand so tightly it hurt.

'Starting tomorrow, you'll go to school there,' Sellass said, when they got close to Mai Bela. 'Tell your teacher. Explain it to her. We do not owe them any money: your school fees are paid until the end of the month.'

Marianna watched as her mother walked off. Then, instead of going to school, she ran back to Edaga Arbi. She didn't want to tell Signora Antonella that she was leaving, she didn't want to have to answer all her classmates' questions. They would want to know why she was abandoning them and she didn't want to have to tell them the truth. She sat next to Zubuc for hours. She felt the warmth of the sun on her skin and tried to revel in the sensation and push away her upsetting thoughts. She spoke softly to the shrub, to the single, yellow variegated leaf that continued to resist the wind. Marianna had buried some tea leaves in the soil around his base, and a new bud had appeared on one of his branches. She also noticed with joy that the tiny birds, Zubuc's friends, had started coming back to visit the shrub every day, chirping noisily around his ailing branches.

When the sun finally went down and the day came to an end, a day so bleak that Marianna had not even wanted to count her thoughts, she told her brother that she had to go to see Tedla and bring him the cigarette butt she had found and saved for him.

Marianna never walked through the village after sundown. There were no lights and she was scared by the shadows and noises of the night. But for some reason she suddenly wanted to visit Tedla. She knew he stayed in his spot until late at night.

The old man's eyes were half shut. He moved his lips without making a sound. A scratchy, moth-eaten blanket was draped over his shoulders.

He had built a small fire with some twigs and it crackled and snapped in front of him. Marianna sat down on the ground by his side and handed him the cigarette butt, which he promptly lit. The mad old man and the little girl stared at the fire without speaking. Sparks flew up into the sky, flickered in the dark and then disappeared. Marianna saw fabulous visions take shape in the bonfire's tiny messengers before they faded: the sparks held forests and flame-coloured castles, they communicated magical stories to the darkness. The old man also watched the small lights take flight. When the last spark died out, Tedla, holding the lit cigarette butt between two fingers, started drawing circles with it in the air, creating a different luminous vision for Marianna. The fiery path enchanted her; Tedla's hand circled faster and faster until it exploded into an endless number of sparks, each one chasing the one ahead of it without ever catching up. When the cigarette went out, Tedla whispered something, and Marianna patted his shoulder gently.

'I have to go now,' she said. 'I have to be home before my mother comes back.'

Tedla nodded and smiled. His white beard rested on his chest, his long hair fell over his shoulders as if to keep him warm. As she ran home, Marianna talked to herself to chase away her fears. She told Elsa what she was thinking, how she had gone to see Tedla, how the sparks were filled with magical tales.

All of a sudden, she heard someone breathing, and she was afraid. Then, in the dark, she recognised Ras, the mangy old dog who sat in the sunny spot where Elsa once cooked injera.

'Ras,' she whispered, patting his head. 'You scared me.'

The dog whimpered and rubbed his nose on the little girl's dress. Then he started limping along beside her. Marianna felt protected.

Once, she had seen Ras bare his teeth and growl at a woman who wanted to chase him away from his place in the sun; the woman ran off in fear and Marianna was proud of the dog. She realised that he did not want her to cross the village on her own in the dark.

When they reached the gate, Marianna said goodbye to Ras. She promised him that she'd give him a piece of her injera the following day. She saw his yellow eyes glow brightly in the dark. The shape of the dog was gone, erased by the darkness, but his eyes continued to shine.

That night a strong wind blew through the village. It whistled and shook their shoddy homes, making its way into every crack and gap. It swept up all the stars into one big pile and tossed them down into the dark chasms.

Marianna and Gianfranco curled up close to their mother in bed. They were scared that they would all be blown away, together with the house, by the crazed wind. It rattled the front gate and door and shook the window, which Sellass had blocked shut with a piece of rooftile.

At dawn, the wind sighed deeply and then disappeared.

That day, the air in the village was calm and clear. Here and there, a few birds lay on the ground, their wings tucked beneath them: the wind had left its mark.

Tedla did not return to his usual sunny spot. He was never seen again. Marianna concluded that the wind had come to carry Tedla back to the village where he had lived as a child, so he could be return to his home, friends and family, finding them just as he had left them so many years earlier.

Indeed, the wind had rebuilt Tedla's village and then hidden it in a deep cavern, to protect it from the passing of time. And now it wanted to give it back to Tedla. The old man went back to being a child: he sat on a boulder and marvelled at the clouds, the sheer rock faces and the birds with multicoloured wings. That child knew nothing of the old man who had once sat in a sunny spot in Edaga Arbi, or how ice crystals had formed in his white beard on the coldest of nights.

When Miezlal, the pretty shepherdess with golden eyes, called to him from across the valley to play with the echo,

Tedla felt strangely confused and wounded. He could not hold on to the memory for long, it kept fading, just like the echo.

He was in another world now, and Miezlal was speaking to him. There were sparks, and then darkness.

30

Gianfranco was eight years old when he left school for good. Suor Giuseppina had said that she was fed up with him, that he was lazy, which was why he was repeating the year. Gianfranco got to his feet, tore his notebook into tiny pieces, heaped them into a tidy pile on his desk, slipped his pencil in his pocket and walked out. Suor Giuseppina and his classmates could only watch in amazement. Zemeth, the deaf girl who worked as a janitor – she adored Gianfranco and constantly tried to communicate with him, making only garbled sounds that got drowned out by the noises from the playground – ran after him, grabbed his arm and tried to make him stay.

Gianfranco looked at Zemeth, watching her lips moving in vain as she tried to express her devotion to him, wriggled out of her grasp, whispered farewell and fled into the street.

For the first time in a long time, Gianfranco felt happy. He looked at the cloudless blue sky, the palm trees on the main avenue, people walking by, and the tall clock tower, and everything seemed new to him, as if he had woken up from a long sleep and was seeing the small bright city for the first time.

He thought of his mother. The evening before, he had told her that he wanted to start working, that he could be a shoe-shine boy or do some other job. Sellass got angry at him and said that she didn't want her son to be a shoe-shine boy; she wanted him to study.

Gianfranco was happy with his decision to leave school. He would never have to set eyes on Suor Giuseppina or be in that classroom, where he had always felt like he was suffocating, ever again.

He walked up and down the avenue several times, then turned up a side road and stopped outside a building from which he heard a strange buzzing sound. The metal shutter was rolled up and inside was a carpentry workshop. A tall, heavy man with reddish hair and a long moustache was smoothing something with a plane. The floor was covered with wood shavings. On the windowsill lay a cat with fur the same orangey-red as the carpenter's hair. It appeared to be sleeping but occasionally opened its eyes, thin green slits, and glanced around to make sure that everything was under control, that nothing would disturb its daily rest. When the cat saw the little boy, it stared at him suspiciously for a moment, and then it went back to purring.

The carpenter continued to work with the plane, large curls of wood falling to the floor, adding to the ones already there.

Gianfranco stood there without saying a word, chewing on what was left of his thumbnail. The man looked up from his work, a piece of wood in his hand.

'What do you want?' he asked gruffly.

'I want to work here,' Gianfranco said, looking into the giant man's eyes.

The man looked at the little boy, noticing his green eyes, dark skin and golden blond hair.

'Work here?' he asked in amazement. 'But I don't need a kid.'

Gianfranco bounced into action as if there were a spring hidden somewhere deep inside him, gathering up all the curls of wood and placing them in a large bag that rested against the wall.

'I can clean the floor, see? I can do anything you need,' he said, coming up to the plane and touching it with a finger. 'I want to learn,' he added.

The man was amazed at the small, scrawny boy's energy. In a fraction of a second, like a spinning top, he had cleared away all the shavings.

'Fine,' the man said, returning to the plane. 'Come back tomorrow morning at eight o'clock.'

Gianfranco picked up a curl that he had missed, tossed it into the sack and ran out. He ran all the way back to Edaga Arbi, waving his arms above his head periodically to harness more strength, feeling like he could fly, as if his arms had become wings.

It was market day in the village. He ran straight through it, bumping into a woman who was setting up her piles of charcoal. She yelled at him, thinking he was a thief, and called to her neighbour to run after him, but the man just shrugged; the child was already gone. Gianfranco ran into the house and flopped down on the ground, covered in sweat. Marianna was not there. Friday was her 'day for the crazies,' when she went to Amba Galliano to talk to the patients at the mental hospital and visit the cemetery across the street from it. Gianfranco knew all about Marianna's strange friends like Lemlem, the young woman who had asked Marianna to bring her some dead people from the cemetery across the street because she was lonely and sad that she did not know their names. Marianna had explained to Lemlem that the dead were afraid of the world of the living because they were no longer used to it; they could only send messages; they'd never leave their homes or cross the street to visit the hospital gardens.

That evening, while Sellass was removing her futah and Marianna was sitting on the floor and writing in her notebook, Gianfranco announced that he had found a job.

Sellass looked at him for a long time without saying a word. She was very tired.

'You have to study,' she said softly. 'You can't leave school.'

'I will not go back to the nuns,' Gianfranco said, stressing each one of his words carefully, giving them importance. 'Tomorrow I start work as a carpenter's assistant. And then we will buy a house.' He glanced at his sister with a challenging look in his eyes and she stared back at him with concern. He did not like being observed in that way, not knowing what she was thinking. 'The carpenter even makes coffins,' he said, trying to impress her, knowing she had just returned from a visit to the cemetery.

'Quiet now,' Sellass said, her head in her hands. 'I don't want to hear another word. Go to sleep.'

Gianfranco crawled under the covers, pulled the blanket over his head, curled up on his side of the bed, and fell asleep immediately.

In his dream, Edaga Arbi was deserted and silent, as if it had been abandoned forever by all of its inhabitants. A few thin coils of fog rose up from the red earth. One after the other, forming a procession, they advanced slowly down the path that led to Acria. Gianfranco knew that those white coils – floating, practically dancing, through the air – were souls that had left their dead bodies. Marianna had told him about souls and how far they needed to travel before reaching the heavenly lands.

Then the souls changed into curls of wood, and Gianfranco saw the big man standing in the middle of the room with his plane.

'Be here tomorrow at eight o'clock,' the carpenter said kindly. 'We have a lot to do. There will be many souls.'

31

Sciusciu the hen, the final survivor of a cheerful brigade of birds that had ended up in the stew pot, hopped around the henhouse, frighted by the unexpected visit from the little girl who came in and sat down in the corner. Once reassured of the visitor's intentions – the girl did not move – she turned her vacuous eyes elsewhere and began to nervously peck at the ground. Her small anaemic egg, the hen's daily offering to the nuns, sat, cold, in a scant pile of straw; it did not appear to Sciusciu that the child was there for that.

Marianna hugged her knees to her chest, trying to warm herself up while thinking of a possible ending to a dramatic story about kidnapped children that she was in the midst of inventing. In the meantime, she kept an eye on the door, waiting for Suor Ernesta to come out for her usual inspection of the garden.

Marianna hoped that the sight of her sitting in the henhouse would provoke a reaction from the nun; Marianna wanted her to understand that she did not want to spend her free hour in the classroom, that she preferred to be alone.

She stopped mulling over a possible conclusion to her story – she would do it later, maybe even give it a happy ending – and thought instead about her relationship with Suor Ernesta.

When she first started going to school in Acria, she brought some small pieces of paper with her, the kind she cut out of packing paper, and one of those notepads that said 'Import-Export' on it, which Sellass somehow managed to procure for her. Signora Antonella had never commented on her paper or notepads, but Suor Ernesta immediately rebuked her, saying she needed a proper notebook and not 'that stuff.'

Back then, her class in the small Acria school was made up of a number of other girls, both mixed-race and Italian, and while some of the nuns distinguished between them, preferring the white girls and even giving them their own table at lunch, Marianna never had any problems with any of her classmates.

Over time, however, almost all the white girls left the school because they were unhappy with it. Now, in Marianna's class, there were only five other little girls, all mixed-race. They did not even bother sitting down properly for lunch anymore. Each of them brought a sandwich from home or a piece of injera. Those with nothing to eat walked around the courtyard, far from the others.

Marianna was a bright student and had no difficulty learning her lessons, but ever since she and Suor Ernesta first met, an obstinate silence had existed between them.

Sometimes the little girl noticed the nun looking at her, scrutinising her, staring at her suspiciously; Marianna had always returned her gaze with a sense of pride. Now and then she wished she could confide in the woman, find some support, and not feel so lonely, but her words always died inside her whenever the nun approached.

She tried to impress her by doing her homework carefully and by writing long and creative compositions, but the nun never said a thing and merely scribbled a good grade in her notebook. During her first year in Acria, the nun had seen her helping a classmate on a test. 'You're a bad girl,' the nun had said to her. 'Tonight the devil will come and drag you away by the feet.'

Ever since then, Marianna was afraid that the dark lord with horns and red eyes would come for her, so she slept with her knees practically touching her chin. Gradually she grew accustomed to how Suor Ernesta repeatedly evoked the devil to keep the image alive in the minds of the youngest girls. Still, Marianna preferred to cover her head, sleep with her knees up to her chest, and when she seemed to hear the devil breathing nearby, she would make the sign of the cross to try to exorcise it.

That morning, Marianna had felt sadder than usual, practically willing to die for Suor Ernesta's attention. And so she had decided to temporarily segregate herself in the henhouse to surprise the nun. Of course, the woman might get angry with her but, at the same time, she would be forced to think about her and how she had chosen to isolate herself there. Anything could happen: they might even make peace and embrace, which would be the perfect ending – Marianna thought – to their sad and silent story.

Suor Ernesta came outside, checked to make sure her heavy set of keys was attached to her belt, and headed towards the garden. She walked past the chicken coop, saw Marianna sitting there, but was not at all fazed. She did, however, peer into the corner to make sure that Marianna had not taken Sciusciu's daily egg. A few minutes later, Suor Ernesta returned from her visit to the vegetable garden, staring straight ahead, ignoring the henhouse altogether.

Marianna continued to sit in the corner without moving, then threw a few pebbles at Sciusciu, who took offence and flew up onto a perch. When the bell rang, Marianna walked out and back to the classroom.

A few days later, Suor Aurelia died. A kind and elderly nun with a cheerful and distracted manner, she had always pinched Marianna's cheeks and called her 'bella bambina.'

More than once, Marianna had tried speaking to the nun, grateful for her kind ways, but the elderly woman was terribly deaf. She would cup her hand around her ear and try to understand what was being said to her, only to then shake her head in resignation. Marianna, humbled by the incommunicable situation, would merely kiss the sister's habit and marvel at how sharp the old woman's eyes were, despite the fact that she looked like a wrinkled old apple.

On her final morning, Suor Aurelia could not get out of bed. She had smiled and said that she was worn out by age, that her time had come. She had rested her head back on the cushion and said a prayer. Then she had closed her eyes, taken one long deep breath to savour what remained of life, and expired.

After keeping vigil over Suor Aurelia during the night, kissing her small cold hands which held her rosary, the little mixed-race girls left, shortly before dawn, to help with the funeral Mass. A young priest from the Comboni mission had come to their small church in Acria to officiate.

Marianna, who was terribly sleepy, did everything she could to keep her eyes open during the service. But the dim light, the flickering candles and the sad hymns sung by the young nuns all had a hypnotic effect on her, and she was drawn into a world of confused dreams.

Barely moving her lips, she tried to pray for the soul that was already travelling across space, having left the diminutive body behind on earth, where it would shrivel up, all alone. But the warmth made her drowsy, her eyes started to close, the sounds of the words grew confused, and the brightly flickering candles looked like all the souls she wanted to think about.

When the priest, followed by the altar boys, started to sing *Dies irae* and came down the few steps from the altar to bless the coffin, Marianna noticed his pleasant face and distinct features in the dim candlelight, but then the smell of the incense increased her torpor and the priest grew hazy.

Later, while Marianna was standing in the courtyard, taking deep breaths of the crisp morning air to banish the sluggishness that had clouded her thinking, Padre Gabriele came up to her, followed by Suor Ernesta. He looked at Marianna carefully and kindly, unlike the nuns, as if he was trying to understand her. She looked back at him tacitly. Suddenly, she felt at peace.

Padre Gabriele asked her a few questions.

'Another abandoned child,' Suor Ernesta interrupted him to say. 'Same old story.'

'Please, Suora,' Padre Gabriele said, holding up his hand, showing the nun that he did not appreciate her interruption.

'I'm not an abandoned child,' Marianna said proudly. 'I live with my mother and brother in Edaga Arbi.'

'Edaga Arbi?' Padre Gabriele asked with grave concern. 'I was there a few days ago. That's hardly a...' He did not finish his sentence. Instead he changed the subject and talked about other things.

'Goodbye Marianna,' he came and said to her later. 'I will return to Acria. You're an intelligent child and I'm certain that you'll pass your exams with high marks.'

Marianna felt Padre Gabriele's deep and low voice resonate through her and settle in a corner of her mind. Now that it was part of her memory, she would be able to recall it whenever she wanted. She tried to hear what Padre Gabriele said to Suor Ernesta as he was leaving, but she could only make out indistinct sounds.

She thought about him for the rest of the day, confident that she had made a new friend.

32

Sellass was dusting the shelf that held Signora Giustina's perfume bottles, all set tidily in a row. As she was wiping down the mirror, she suddenly stopped, arm raised, and looked at her reflection.

It felt like she was looking at a stranger, as if someone else was staring back at her, wondering what she was doing there. It was a strange sensation, as if in that exact second, in that house, she, Sellass, was nothing more than an invention of that passing moment in time.

Her head started spinning and she brought her hand to her forehead. The evening before she had beaten Marianna hard, striking her face, shoulders and back, then she had pushed her down onto the floor. There had been no real reason, she just couldn't control herself. She returned every evening to that squalid room, tired and depressed, only to find the children part of the squalor; every evening they were there waiting for her, small and scrawny, always shivering. It felt like her entire life story was written in their sorrowful eyes.

Gianfranco had told her, with the boldness of a small man, that he wanted to keep a little money so that he could buy himself an ear of corn on his way home from work in the evening. He had rights too, he had said, looking at his mother and biting his nails. He worked twelve hours a day, and on Saturdays he brought home a 'tip.' Hardly anything, Sellass thought with a heavy sigh, reflecting on the fact that her son built coffins for the dead. But at least he was learning a trade, and that giant of a man, the owner of the workshop, whom she'd seen once while passing by, did not seem to be unkind. Maybe one day she'd be able to convince Gianfranco to go back to school. He was the son of a white man, after all, he shouldn't have to go through life without an education.

Then Marianna had told her mother that Suor Ernesta wanted to talk to her, that she needed to come to her school. So Sellass had beaten her and told her she was a bad girl, or why else would Suor Ernesta have asked Sellass to come to the school. Sometimes, when she looked at her daughter, she felt the whole world explode.

Marianna had not gone straight to bed, hiding under the covers and crying, as she usually did. She had walked out, slammed the door behind her, and gone to sit with Zubuc, who was covered in countless shiny new buds and seemed proud of how he had returned to his past splendour after his close scrape with death.

'I need some magic, too,' Marianna had whispered to the plant in tears. 'I want to get away from here. And if my mother doesn't change, I'll leave her.'

Marianna had noticed the shrub quiver as if communicating with her but maybe it had just been a soft gust of wind that had rustled through the branches. The tender green buds were like so many little eyes, all looking at Marianna and beyond, deep into the night.

Then Marianna had walked back to the doorway and stared long and hard at her mother. Sellass had never seen her daughter look at her like that.

'You hate me,' Marianna had said. 'I'm going to get away from here as soon as I possibly can.'

In the meantime, Sellass had calmed down. She went and sat down on the angareb and looked at her bare feet. 'You have to realise that all these objects that you talk to will never actually help you,' she said to Marianna. 'You need to start thinking straight. You have to stop wandering around. You're not some poor girl from Edaga Arbi. Do you understand? We'll leave this place soon,' Sellass had said. Then, as in all difficult moments, came the query. 'How could he…?'

Sellass realised, as she thought back to the prior evening, that she would never have a good relationship with Marianna. Just then, Signora Giustina walked into the bathroom.

'What? Still here? You ought to have finished with the bathroom by now!' she snapped.

Sellass looked at the Signora's sleepy face, the hairnet that she wore to keep her curlers in place and her long soft bathrobe.

'Why are you looking at me like that?' Giustina lashed out. 'Get a move on!'

Sellass collected her cleaning tools and left the bathroom.

That night, as she was walking home, she saw a man waiting for her. He was Eritrean and wore an elegant pinstripe suit that accentuated his handsome build.

'My name is Marcos,' he said. 'Zegai told me that you want to buy a house.'

Sellass stopped and leant against a lamppost, covering part of her face with her futah. 'Yes,' she said. 'I think I have saved up enough money.'

'I can ask around for you,' the man said, stepping closer, almost touching her. 'There's something for sale in Ghezzabanda.'

'I don't want to live in Ghezzabanda,' Sellass said.

'It's a nice area, much better than Edaga Arbi.'

'Anything is better than Edaga Arbi. I want to buy a house in a place that I like.'

'We can discuss it,' Marcos said, starting to look uncomfortable. 'Some time ago I told Zegai that I might be able to help you. You're still young,' he said, gently lifting the futah off her face.

Sellass could smell and feel his breath on her skin. She looked at Marcos' hands, clean and smooth. She felt them on her shoulders and neck, strong and warm. They gave her a sense of wellbeing. She closed her eyes, saw the angareb on the terrace of the house on the salt flats, and imagined the feel of Carlo's body.

'Sellass, Sellass,' Marcos whispered softly and intensely, reminding her of how the sea had spoken to her in that long-ago dream that she had recounted to Mariam.

When Marcos' hands touched her breasts, Sellass felt the desire to draw him closer.

Suddenly, she took a few steps back. 'Tell me how much it will cost. How much will you charge to find a house for me? I want to live in Amba Galliano.' She drew the futah back over her face, leaving only her kohl-lined eyes visible, dark and shiny. 'And there will be nothing else. Do you understand me?'

Marcos wrung his hands together and thought for a moment. 'Fine, Sellass,' he said, imitating her arrogant tone of voice. 'You tell me how much you want to spend and I'll tell you what my rate is. Or else you can find another intermediary. There are lots of them out there. Even your boss could find you one.'

'Goodnight,' the woman whispered and continued home to Edaga Arbi.

When she walked into the house, she pulled a small bundle of papers out of her dress and went directly over to Marianna, who sat reading an old newspaper that she had found in the rubbish.

'Tell me what these papers say,' she said, holding them out to her daughter.

Marianna read the numbers out loud several times. Sellass sat on the mat with her eyes shut, her lips moving, trying to follow the numbers that crowded her head.

'Good,' Sellass said, taking back the papers.

The next day, before dawn, Sellass accompanied her daughter to school in Acria, even though she had no desire to see the nun who had humiliated her.

Suor Ernesta came to the gate and greeted Sellass with a quick nod. Her eyes, behind her thick eyeglasses, seemed to get smaller and smaller the more she tried to focus on the woman standing in front of her.

'Cut your daughter's hair,' she said. 'She stinks of Abyssinian butter.'

Marianna looked down at the ground. She focused on the laces of her worn-out shoes.

'Fine,' Sellass said. 'Anything else?'

To the child, the silence that hung in the air after her mother asked that question felt like a condemnation. Suor Ernesta prolonged it even further before speaking.

'People like you need to learn humility,' the nun finally

said. 'Do you know what humility is?' she asked and then sighed, touching the crucifix that hung from her belt.

Sellass stared at her and said nothing.

'Never mind,' Suor Ernesta brought their conversation to an end. 'Take her to have her hair cut. I do not want to see that braid any longer. And pray, both of you.'

The following morning Marianna and her mother set out for Abbashawel, a village comprised of tukuls and shacks where many Eritreans lived. In those years, in fact, most of the local population lived in Abbashawel. White people never went near that poverty-stricken and ill-famed neighbourhood. Sellass and Marianna would go to see Neghissi, the elderly woman who cut hair with shards of glass and did braids for the Eritrean women.

In the spectral light of early dawn, as the night was fading but before the sun had risen, Sellass and Marianna arrived at a massive plaster wall that was still under construction, part of a large building that marked the entrance to the village. Standing at the unfinished wall, slapping it with their hands, were countless little girls dressed in rags the colour of sand.

In the quiet of the still-sleeping neighbourhood, the sound of their hands smacking the plaster was constant and endless, like a giant, invisible clock obsessively ticking away the seconds.

White powder fell from above onto the girls' faces and clothes, forming soft carpets at their feet. The children, wiry figures that leant into the wall, looked like tortured souls banging on the door to a world they would never be allowed to enter. The white powder continued to fall, clouds filled the air, turning the children's black hair white and ethereal, leaving them faceless. They did not speak, they never turned around, they just kept slapping the wall.

Marianna squeezed her mother's hand tightly. She had questions but did not dare ask them. It felt as though just by being there she had desecrated a world that did not belong to her, and she was afraid that the little girls would turn around and notice her.

'Come,' Sellass whispered and shortly afterwards they entered Neghissi's tukul.

'Who are they?' Marianna asked, tipping her head in the direction of the girls.

Neghissi sat down on the ground, laid out her bottle shards, and brushed her teeth with a wooden stick.

'They're Agame,' she said with a shrug. 'They come from far away to look for work and when they get here they seem more dead than alive. Many older men take them in, and then send them to work at the mill; with all the hardship we have, they certainly can't maintain them.'

'And they stand there slapping the stone wall all day?' Marianna asked uneasily.

'Yes,' Neghissi said, sharpening her shards. 'They're used to it. And when the sun goes down, they gather up the flour and bring it home.'

'I need you to cut my daughter's hair,' Sellass said. 'The nun told me to do it and we have to do whatever she says. Marianna has to stay in that school. She has to study.'

'I see,' Neghissi said. 'She is not an Agame.'

First, the woman used a shard to sever Marianna's braid. The child watched as it fell to the mat and lay there immobile, forever detached from her, a dead object, no longer able to take those deep breaths that had once electrified each and every strand, no longer able to stand on end after the rare occasions she was able to wash her hair.

Then Neghissi started to cut the hair on her head. Marianna felt the shard scrape across her scalp, scratching her, she wanted to scream but bit her lip and swallowed her pain. She didn't want to show any sign of weakness to her mother, ever. Eventually her head was bare except for some clots of dried blood and a few rebellious locks that managed to dodge the glass. Sellass handed the woman a coin and said nothing.

On their way back to Acria it was hard for Marianna not to break down and cry. She thought of her braid, all alone, far away, abandoned on a garbage heap visited by hyenas; she thought of the little Agame girls who slapped the wall every day and lived with men who were not their relatives; she thought of Abbashawel, it was almost worse than Edaga Arbi.

She thought of what her life would be like if she had to slap a wall every day for hours on end and could never look at the world around her, what it would feel like to have flour fall onto her face and body, the endless smacking sound her only company. She thought of her embarrassment, how her classmates would comment on her shaved head, how Suor Ernesta could never go to hell because she was a nun.

When she walked into class, her head covered with the kerchief that Elsa had given her, she felt all the girls' eyes on her. It lasted only a second. Then they all pretended to look down at their notebooks, which lay open in front of them.

'Good morning, Marianna,' the nun said with a hint of a smile. 'Don't you feel better now?'

It seemed to Marianna that the nun's small eyes sparkled with satisfaction at seeing her poor, shaved head.

'Yes, I do,' she replied firmly. She did not want Suor Ernesta to think that she felt in the least bit humiliated.

The nun told the class to write an essay; the title was 'Describe your home.'

Marianna chewed on her pencil for a moment, then looked around at the other girls. They were writing slowly, turning to look at her every so often. She was always the first to finish and was usually glad to give them ideas about what to write.

Her scalp burned. All she could see were the little Agame girls, the way Suor Ernesta looked at her, and how her mother beat her. She wished she could get up and leave, the way Gianfranco had, or become a bush, like Zubuc; she would have made all the little strawberry finches so happy.

Her home had two angarebs, a frayed straw mat, holes in the roof, and a rickety door and window. If she were to describe the spiderweb or her friend Zubuc, Suor Ernesta would not understand. She could hardly write about the one ray of sunshine that toyed with the darkness in the corner, or about the ants and how they carried pieces of straw that were so much larger than they were, or about the stars that came to visit the courtyard each night. Marianna picked up her blank sheet of paper, folded it as instructed, got to her feet and handed it to the nun.

33

Egisto, the electrician known to everyone in Asmara, lived in a small, cheerful house in Amba Galliano. He worked hard until five o'clock on Friday evening, when he closed up shop and drove to Agordat in his little car. He spent his weekends on the low plains, hunting wild animals and pretty teenage girls who filled his dreams. He had fathered a little girl with one of them, who now lived with her mother in Tessenei, a village where there were other Europeans.

One evening, just beyond Keren, as he was driving along and thinking about Shezar, the girl he had met at the spice market, and her body, so tightly wrapped in a colourful futah, he found the road blocked by several large boulders. He realised immediately that it was an ambush and quickly tried to turn the car around. Three men armed with knives and guns leapt out from behind a giant baobab, shot at the car, forcing him to halt, and then dragged Egisto out of it.

He was terrified. The men – who were tall and skinny and had masses of hair into which were tucked large wooden combs – held him still and talked excitedly among themselves. Egisto could neither move nor call for help. It was as if he had been struck by a sudden paralysis. The only thought he managed to have, in a moment that seemed to last forever, was how absurd it would be for him to be killed by blacks at this point, after choosing to move all the way to Africa so many years earlier. Had it not been for his passion for hunting and for the young girls of the low plains, he'd probably be safe at home in Italy with his wife, who had moved back one year before. He thought of the young man who had been killed by shiftas on the road to Massawa a few months back. People were scared at first, then they called it an isolated incident and everyone had gone back to travelling up and down those roads.

He tried to find the strength to shout for help and defend himself, but it felt like he was made of stone. After beating him up, the men tied him to the baobab tree.

Egisto shut his eyes, sweat ran down his face, his heart beat wildly in his chest. He could imagine the headlines of the paper, chronicling his death: 'Electrician Egisto R., barbarically killed by shiftas on road to Agordat.'

And yet, he felt that it was not his time to die. Death was a sad business, but it was not his time. Not yet. He was about to go hunting, he was about to spend some time with his young girlfriend; Egisto R. was still in the prime of his life. He looked up at the blazing sky and tried to remember a prayer, but he hadn't thought about God in so long, not since he was a child, when he had attended a school run by priests.

Nothing there, in that unique landscape that he so adored, nothing in the peaceful mountains or the vast plains or the endless palm trees, nothing as far as the eye could see rebelled against his death. A flock of birds crossed the sky, their wings shining brilliantly in the final red blaze of the sun.

He heard the sound of life buzzing beneath the rocks and bushes. With night's arrival, he heard the call of a hyena. He was surrounded by calm and tranquillity. Nature breathed in the cool breeze carried there by the evening and was not the least bit interested in Egisto. Confused by his own fear, he felt both wonder and desperation at the great indifference of the world; he felt like he was the only living being on earth and that he deserved to be saved thanks to some miraculous event.

The shiftas tortured him by making him wait. His body was discovered the following day by a shepherd. He had been brutally stabbed to death.

The killing of Egisto caused a great deal of upset and fear. People could no longer ignore the danger presented by the shiftas. And the house in Amba Galliano was put up for sale.

His widow wanted to get rid of the house quickly and signed a proxy allowing someone she knew to sell it fast, even at a modest price. She wanted to sever all ties with Africa.

Padre Gabriele, who knew of Sellass' desire to buy a house in Amba Galliano from Marianna, made his way to Edaga Arbi one Sunday to inform her. He found Gianfranco sitting in the courtyard with his pile of pebbles. The boy looked at Padre Gabriele, nodded in greeting, and started chewing on the skin around his nails.

'Where's your mother?' Padre Gabriele asked Gianfranco, gently tousling the child's hair. Gianfranco seemed unwilling to reply, as if his thoughts were elsewhere. Then he knocked over his tower of pebbles.

'She's not here,' he said.

'And Marianna?'

Gianfranco bit his lip. 'She's at the hospital,' he mumbled. 'She has typhoid.'

Padre Gabriele did his best not to reveal any emotion. He sat down on the ground with the boy and together they rebuilt the tower of pebbles. Then he took a shiny stone out of his pocket and placed it on top. 'This is from the river Barka,' the priest said. 'I'll bring you some more.' He got to his feet and swept the dust off his cassock. 'I'm going to check on Marianna now,' he added. 'And hopefully bring her home soon.'

'What if she dies?' the child whispered, going back to biting his nails.

'Not a chance,' Padre Gabriele said with a smile. 'You're very strong children. Tell your mother that there's a house for sale in Amba Galliano that she might like.'

He drove off, the children from the village chasing after his run-down old car, waving their arms and laughing. He headed to the hospital for the Eritreans; Marianna would be there. It wasn't surprising, he thought to himself as he drove as fast as he could across the rocky and uneven road, that she had come down with typhoid fever. Water was delivered to Edaga Arbi twice a week, it wasn't drinkable but people drank it anyway. Survivors, which is to say anyone who had lived past their first two years of life, could handle all sorts of bacteria. Gianfranco and Marianna had not lived in Edaga Arbi for the first two years of their lives. Padre Gabriele wondered how they had actually survived there at all.

He parked his car in front of the Eritrean hospital and walked rapidly through the main entrance. He asked for Dr. Salvini, a young physician he knew well. The doctor greeted him warmly, like an old friend.

'Her case is serious,' the doctor replied when Padre Gabriele asked about Marianna. 'I don't think she'll make it. Her mother left just a few minutes ago.'

Accompanied by the doctor, Padre Gabriele walked down a dark hallway crowded with people laying on mattresses, making it hard for doctors and nurses to get by, until they reached Marianna. People around her cried out in pain, begged for help, children wailed, and there was an unpleasant odour of illness and disinfectant.

Padre Gabriele knelt down next to the little girl. She was groggy. A small container of water rested nearby.

'We need to move her,' Padre Gabriele said, placing his hand on her sweaty forehead.

'Praise Jesus Christ,' mumbled an old Eritrean nun, coming up to Padre Gabriele. 'She needs the last rites, Padre. It doesn't look like she'll make it through the night.'

Padre Gabriele kept his hand on Marianna's forehead as if transmitting some of his strength to her. He felt the nun staring at him. He didn't want to give her the last rites, he didn't want to accept that she might die.

'Can you find her a better bed?' Padre Gabriele asked the doctor again.

The doctor nodded and said he would have her taken to a proper bed that had just been freed.

'But doctor, that one is already reserved,' a nurse standing nearby said.

'Don't worry,' the doctor replied. 'I'll take care of everything.' He waited until the nurse walked off to explain. 'It's always a problem with mixed-race children. The nurses don't want them here, but they're not welcome at the Italian hospital either. If they don't have their father's last name, they're considered Eritrean and so they get brought here.'

Marianna's forehead was burning hot and she was having a difficult time breathing.

'Anything could happen, Padre,' the nun said. 'But at this point, she really ought to receive the final sacraments.'

Padre Gabriele turned to look at the nun: small in stature, her eyes revealed the sad and resigned gaze of someone who tends to the desperate and dying every single day.

Padre Gabriele sighed and administered the last rites to Marianna.

The following day, Marianna opened her eyes, recognised Padre Gabriele and even smiled at him. She had made it through the critical phase of the illness; the doctor was amazed at the sudden improvement in her condition.

When Marianna had been placed on the mattress on the floor, in that dark hallway that seemed to be filled with spectral forms, she had squeezed her mother's hand tightly and shut her eyes. Sellass was told that she was not allowed to stay in the hospital overnight; before leaving, she had given some coins to a cleaning woman, asking her to check on her daughter often. Then, covering her face with her futah, she had walked out.

Marianna had been frightened: she tried to recall some of her thoughts so she wouldn't feel so alone. But then her fever rose and her thoughts dispersed and got mixed up, creating a blend of images that crowded the dark hallway and joined in the wailing around her.

Marianna saw them gather around her; Elsa and Tedla were there, larger than life, their heads reaching all the way up to the ceiling. She also saw the sea, its waves rose high up in the sky and then rolled towards her, trying to drag her out with them. When only Marianna's shadow remained on the beach, looking around in desperation for her body, which had since been taken out to sea, she caught sight of a little house. It was in Amba Galliano, it had a small garden with a pepper tree, in which sat a *maskal*, its feathers changing colour with each note it sang, from green to orange, until the little bird resembled a tiny ball of fire.

When Marianna saw Padre Gabriele sitting next to her bed, she sighed with relief. Her fears vanished and her thoughts were calmed.

'You're a strong girl, Marianna,' he said. 'We'll have you out of here in a couple of days. Your mother came this morning, before work, but you were still sleeping.'

'I had so many dreams,' Marianna said, calculating that she could now add the house in Amba Galliano and the maskal bird in the pepper tree to her thoughts.

'What kind of dreams did you have?' Padre Gabriele asked, gently smoothing her forehead.

'I dreamt of a house with a garden, and a tree with a maskal in it, and the maskal was singing. It was in Amba Galliano. I even recognised the road, I went down it once while I was out exploring.'

'Sometimes,' Padre Gabriele said in a whisper, as if he wanted his words to remain a secret between them, 'certain dreams come true.'

34

At the break of day, when the first hint of light tentatively appeared in the sky, there was the sound of the muezzin from the white mosque near the market. Then, at six o'clock, the cathedral bells started to ring, and a few elderly ladies in veils slowly made their way up the steps to pray in the Catholic church.

A short Arab man knelt on the ground in front of Sellass' house in Edaga Arbi, raising his arms towards the rising sun and repeating the words of the muezzin.

Sellass opened the gate and waited for the man to finish his prayers before speaking. 'We're ready. We have to leave now,' she said. 'Come in and get our belongings.'

The short man stretched, sniffed a pinch of tobacco and went inside their home. In a matter of minutes he loaded the angareb, and everything else they owned, onto a cart hitched to an old workhorse who stood dreaming of endless fields and fodder. Marianna knelt down on the ground next to Zubuc, gently stroking each and every one of the plant's leaves.

'He's too big to dig up and take with us now,' she said to Gianfranco. 'But I'll come back with someone who can help me.'

'What if he dies?' Gianfranco asked, sleepily sucking his thumb.

'Zubuc won't die, he's magic,' she said boldly, getting up and walking around the courtyard and house as if saying farewell to a thousand invisible things.

The children climbed onto the cart and sat down next to the man. Marianna asked him the horse's name. Sellass sat in the back, between the angarebs, her face covered with her futah.

Slowly the cart crossed the village, its wheels creaking, breaking the early morning silence. A number of women came to the doors of their run-down homes, cleaning their teeth with wooden sticks and staring at the passing exodus. A boy, struggling with a stubborn donkey, spat on the ground when he saw the children.

The cart driver urged the poor horse to walk faster but without much conviction; the animal, ears back and eyes on the ground, seemed to be immersed in his own sad thoughts, as though he had no intention of modifying his sleepy pace. The man knew it was pointless to insist, he had had Sinbad for many years; he was used to showing his clients that his horse was the boss and that he was in no position to order him around. Sinbad, trusting in their long friendship – both were old and weak in the legs, able to communicate with a single glance – let the man's commands hang in the air. The whip, for the horse, was merely a tool for chasing away flies.

Ras, the mangy dog, limped along behind the cart, the children turning around repeatedly to look at him. Marianna hoped the dog would follow them all the way to Amba Galliano and find a new sunny spot there where he could spend his days.

But when they reached the grain market, Ras hesitated, sniffed the air, glanced affectionately at the children and then turned back.

'Maybe he'll join us later,' Marianna said to her brother softly. 'Dogs always know where to find friends.'

'He's old,' Gianfranco said, playing with a balled-up bit of bread. 'And he's blind. He needs to be in Edaga Arbi.'

Marianna turned around one more time to look: Ras was limping back to his spot where he could warm his bones.

When they reached Amba Galliano, the sun was rising and the house was enveloped in silence.

Sellass opened the gate with a key, then used a smaller key to open the front door. She moved fluidly but remained impassive, as if the house had always been hers.

The children followed her indoors and looked around wide-eyed, without daring to speak, as if they had walked into a church.

The two rooms were filled with light, it was a house fit for a party, Marianna thought, noticing the pink walls and how the sun shone on them. There was even a kitchen and a small bathroom.

Sellass gently told the short man to bring their angarebs and other belongings into the house.

The old horse flicked its tail at some flies, enjoying those few peaceful moments and the warm rays of light.

In the garden was a pepper tree and on one of its branches sat a small maskal, its feathers the colour of fire. After hopping about between the leaves, the bird eventually settled on the highest branch, bobbed its head a few times, preened its feathers with its beak, and then, sitting very still, it looked up at the sky and began to sing a clear song of pure joy.

35

A sudden hailstorm fell over the city; the streets emptied out and everything turned white. People rushed home or into bars and cafés. Beggars made their way to their hiding places and held on to each other for dear life, teeth chattering, amazed and frightened by the chunks of ice that fell from the dark sky, creating a lunar landscape that scared away all forms of life. The elderly thought of their fields, how their crops would be destroyed, the constant poverty. Children stared in amazement at the magic that made that day unique. The palm trees and other plants that lined the main streets bowed and quivered under gusts of icy wind. Birds flew off in fear, some were struck by hailstones and fell to the ground, their wings spread wide.

On Viale della Regina, a horse went into a frenzy, whinnying and shaking its mane, desperately trying not to lose its balance, but kicking every which way, making the old buggy to which it was hitched rock violently up and down. Then it took off at a gallop, slid on the ice, crashed heavily into the cathedral wall and fell to the ground.

Suddenly, as if an orchestra conductor had waved his baton to end the music, the hailstorm stopped. The black clouds disappeared beyond the mountains, leaving the sky crystal clear.

Illuminated by the sun, the icy hailstones on the ground glinted with a bluish light, as if the city streets had been strewn with diamonds.

The palm trees extended their wide leaves, all covered with raindrops, each one of them a world of brightness. A single bird sang a tremulous note, calling to its friends to celebrate the end of the storm.

Children came rushing out of their hiding places and invented games with pieces of rapidly melting ice. No one seemed to notice the horse lying on its side in front of the cathedral, its legs broken. But then an old Italian carriage driver, trembling with age and moving with difficulty across the ice, made his way towards his horse, followed by a crowd of Eritrean children.

Marianna stepped out of the foyer of the building where she had sought refuge and continued on to Amba Galliano. She had completed her half day as a seamstress with the Giubelli sisters and in the afternoon she would work at the Comboni mission. Marianna was agile and light and had no difficulty moving across the ice. She had always enjoyed doing balancing acts and surprising Gianfranco with her acrobatics.

She secretly wished that she could have studied dance with Signorina Audasio, like many of the Italian girls did, but she never told anyone because she knew it would never come true: fairy godmothers didn't exist, pumpkins could not be transformed into carriages, Cinderella would never get dressed for a ball. And the thought of praying to God, in whom she deeply believed, for dance lessons was absurd.

The Heavenly Father would not appreciate such a prayer; far more important requests filled the heavens. Even so, Marianna told herself that anything could happen, and she continued to imagine that one day she might dance to 'Swan Lake' in a splendid tulle dress and satin shoes.

As she glided across the ice, fascinated by its sheen, she thought of the fluffy tutus she had seen in the pictures of the latest dance performance, on display in Lusci's photography studio, with all the pretty ballerinas standing on the tips of their toes. Under each of the photos was a caption that seemed, in itself, a fable: 'Swan Lake,' 'The Magic Box,' 'La Danse Macabre.'

Marianna saw the girls who took dance classes, or played tennis at the club, or were part of the volleyball team every single day when they left school: a wave of satchels and pinafores with soft pleats. When the final bell rang, they rose up from their rows like a flock of doves and flew through the air, trilling their afternoon plans, giggling about shared secrets, but never once noticing Marianna as she walked all alone on the other side of the street. It was as if they were from another planet. Actually, Marianna knew all their names and even a little something about each one of them from the Giubelli sisters' workshop, where, in addition to the skirts and blouses, a fair number of stories were also artfully crafted. The two sisters liked to talk about their clients and Marianna always listened, nodding every so often: pretty little Silvana's mother would bring them some taffeta for a special dress that her daughter needed; Clara's heart had been broken for the first time; Lydia would soon have a birthday party at her house.

The sisters would send Marianna out to deliver their work. Standing at the gates to the girls' homes, she often felt intimidated. Sometimes their mothers came out and thanked her and gave her a tip, while other times their Eritrean maids came to the gate and took the packages from her without saying a word.

Marianna had almost reached Amba Galliano when a car pulled up alongside her. She peered in at the young man at the wheel and he smiled at her. It was Gilberto, the son of the paediatrician. Marianna had seen him around, on his way to the Mingardi swimming pool or out with his friends in the evening.

Gilberto was good looking, elegant and had a warm smile. The Giubelli sisters had mentioned that a great many girls were infatuated with him.

'Where are you headed?' Gilberto asked.

Marianna felt uncomfortable and wished she could run away.

'I'm going home,' she said, speaking gruffly to conceal her emotions.

Gilberto turned off the engine and looked around to make sure that no one was watching.

'Can I see you tonight?' he asked.

Marianna stared at the clumps of grass poking through the melting ice, dripping with moisture. Here and there were puddles, each one holding a bit of sky. Invisible insects had softly started playing their concerts once again.

'I can't,' she whispered. It hardly seemed possible that Gilberto wanted to spend time with her.

'Why not?' he asked, still smiling, his gaze simple and serene. 'I'll wait for you here at seven o'clock,' he added when she did not reply. 'I'd like to talk to you. I like you.' And with that, Gilberto waved goodbye and drove back down to town.

Marianna entered her house, flustered. She sat down in her usual spot near the window that looked out on the pepper tree. She thought of her mother. Sellass had always told her to be careful and wary of any invitations that she would surely receive from men and boys. But Sellass was always grumpy and wary of everyone. Marianna could never talk to her mother about such things; she wanted to get away from her, to leave.

Marianna had stopped going to school when she turned eleven because she wanted to become independent as quickly as possible. The nuns had agreed with her decision, saying that it was good that she start to work, that other girls were better suited to studying.

She learned how to cut and sew fabric from the nuns at the Comboni mission. The Giubelli sisters had her work with them in the morning hours and gave her lunch, nothing more. They said it was hard for them, too, that they could not afford to hire her full-time. The younger sister, who was as skinny as a twig that had never sprouted leaves, was a spinster; the older sister, cheerful enough but prone to extreme mood swings, had lost her husband in an English prison camp in South Africa. She had two children to take care of and Marianna understood her situation. Like her, those children were growing up fatherless.

Marianna received a modest salary from the nuns at the Comboni mission and always used a little of her earnings to buy a small bar of soap, a tube of toothpaste, or a bottle of shampoo. She took good care of her body and long hair. The Edaga Arbi days, when the nuns said her hair stank like Abyssinian butter, were long gone.

Marianna's dream was to leave Asmara and find a new world in Italy, the land of her father. Before leaving Edaga

Arbi, Marianna had found a document, hidden inside one of her mother's cloth bags, in which a man named Carlo Cinzi declared that she and Gianfranco were his children. She wrote down the details in one of her secret notebooks, but then the cloth bag and the document had disappeared; Marianna wasn't sure if Sellass had hidden it again or if it had been lost in the move. Either way, now she knew her father's real name and that he had written down on a piece of paper that he was the father of Sellass' two children.

In those few minutes when she ought to have been resting, but when so many other thoughts crowded her brain, she wondered who exactly her father was – the man who had disappeared into nothingness. When she rooted around in the dark for memories, she saw pink flamingos flying across the sky and then a kite, she seemed to hear a voice and smell the sea and its warmth, but then everything went dark again, and no matter how hard she tried, she could not find the image she was looking for. She thought about Gianfranco's big green eyes and his blond hair, which were surely those of their father, and she tried to find him in the chaos, but the memory of his face was not there.

Then the thought of meeting Gilberto came back to her. First she shivered with excitement and then felt warmth rush to her head. The hours that she had to spend at the Comboni mission before their meeting would feel endless.

She had seen many girls of fifteen, her age, strolling up and down the Corso in the evening with their sweethearts. Sometimes she even saw couples turn down dark, empty streets and disappear.

When she walked down the Corso in the evening, always staying off to one side, she liked watching people. The girls were like bellflowers: their petals opening up as the day cooled down, releasing their intense perfumes. She wondered if one day she, too, might walk down the streets in the centre of town with a special someone.

She left the mission in a hurry that evening, after asking the sisters for permission to leave five minutes early so she could take care of an urgent errand. She changed out of her work uniform and put on the modest, light blue cotton dress that she wore on special occasions, which Sellass had asked the usual Yemeni tailor to make for her, and, after redoing her braid, she set out for her date.

Gilberto drove off in the direction of Keren, but then stopped on the side of the road. With those quiet, dark and majestic gorges nearby, Marianna felt like she could practically hear the twinkling of the stars: there were so many of them and they huddled so close together, filling every inch of the sky. She saw the moon rising: large and round, it struggled to find a place among all the stars, illuminating the night with a golden glow. Marianna felt terribly excited.

She did not know what to say. She tried to find words but none came to her. It was hard to breathe. Then Gilberto kissed her, touched her body, and told her they could see each other often, at night. Marianna wanted to tell him that she'd like to walk down the Corso with him, but she didn't say a word.

When Gilberto tried to pull up her dress, she pushed him away brusquely.

'What do I have to do, beg you?' Gilberto said, gripping her arm with force. 'Or is there something else you want?'

'Take me home,' Marianna whispered, at the same time opening the car door. 'Or I'll walk home.'

'The hyenas would eat you,' he said with a smirk. 'Are you sure you don't want anything? I can give you presents, you know.'

'I want to go home.'

'Fine,' Gilberto said, turning on the engine. 'There are plenty of girls just like you, over by the market, at night. And none of them act the way you do.'

They drove back without talking.

'You had nothing to lose, you know,' Gilberto said when she got out of the car. 'If you change your mind, let me know.'

That night, Marianna couldn't sleep. She realised that Gilberto would never walk down the Corso with her. He would keep her a secret, as if he were ashamed of her. It was humiliating. Her thoughts went back to her father and how he had abandoned Sellass and his children. Then she thought about Giulia, the girl she had often seen out walking with Gilberto. What an awful girl, Marianna thought. Tall, slender, with an upturned nose and dark bob, always well dressed in perfectly ironed, pleated skirts and soft woollen sweaters, she walked down the street as if only she existed. Marianna wondered what Giulia would say if she found out that Gilberto was fooling around with mulatto girls.

The following day Marianna didn't go home during her lunch break. She needed to walk as far as she could, tire herself out. It was the only way she could find some peace. She could go as far as the mental hospital, or to the cemetery in Ghezzabanda, or she could walk up and down the steps where the cripples gathered. She thought about Edaga Arbi. She did not want to go back there. She had only returned there once since they had moved, to uproot Zubuc, but he was gone. In his place she found only a patch of dry earth.

'What are you looking for?' asked the elderly beggar who lived there with a blind man.

'A friend,' she had replied.

'A friend?' the old man had asked with surprise.

'Yes,' Marianna had continued to stare at the red earth where there was no sign of Zubuc. 'A bush.'

The old man had shaken his head. 'I never saw a bush growing there. See how dry the earth is? Nothing can grow there.'

'But that's where he grew,' Marianna had replied, her voice breaking with emotion. 'Somehow he always managed not to die.'

Marianna had leant on the rickety metal gate and shut her eyes. Zubuc was happy, happier than he had ever been. He was happy that his little friend had left Edaga Arbi and gone to live in a house in Amba Galliano. He was so happy that all his branches had turned into wings. And because he did not want to stay in that squalid place all alone, he had flown away with the little strawberry finches perched on him like colourful chirping flowers. He had flown far away towards the garden of his dreams.

Now, when Marianna thought of Zubuc, she felt that he was part of her. And despite feeling very different from the young white people who strolled up and down the Corso, she felt something resonate deep inside her that brought her great joy. It was as if she had sprouted a branch of her own. Marianna took a deep breath; she could practically swallow the clear early-afternoon light.

36

Once their governing mandate came to an end, the English left Eritrea and the country became independent. Around that same time, the Italian government issued a decree regarding Italian-Eritreans: legally recognised children born to couples comprised of an Italian parent and an Eritrean one could obtain Italian citizenship. If the child's biological parent chose not to recognise their offspring, any Italian citizen could offer their last name to the mixed-race child. As a result, many such children, abandoned and never legally recognised by their fathers, tried, with all means possible, to obtain an Italian last name.

Marianna thought a great deal about her last name – it would permit her to go to Italy one day – and she always listened carefully to the nuns when they talked quietly, while sewing, about this or that kind-hearted man who had offered to recognise a child as his own. A few of them shook their heads sceptically. 'Let's hope the poor man doesn't have problems down the road,' they often said.

Marianna did not want to ask the nuns for help but she spoke to Padre Gabriele about the piece of paper that she had found while they were moving. Padre Gabriele discussed the document with Sellass, pointing out that it would help to officialise Marianna and Gianfranco's position in society.

Sellass listened quietly, staring into the distance. She then dismissed Padre Gabriele curtly by saying that she had never had such a document, that Marianna was wrong.

Padre Gabriele struggled to understand Sellass' attitude – she was clearly lying – and he suggested to Marianna that she be patient, that he would look into things for her.

Suddenly, however, Padre Gabriele had to leave for Italy, called back by his superiors to Rome, and he did not know when he would return. Marianna, who continued to think about her last name, decided to find someone willing to give her one. She did not understand why her mother had not saved that piece of paper – Padre Gabriele did not tell Marianna that Sellass had denied its very existence – and, unable to broach the topic directly with her, she felt her bitterness and desire to leave her mother grow stronger. She tried to convince Gianfranco to do something to obtain an Italian last name, to talk about it with the carpenter, but her brother just looked at her with his sad, bewildered gaze and went back to his hobby of building strange, complex contraptions and then patiently taking them apart.

One Sunday, Marianna, who could not think of anything else – forgetting even Gilberto, whose handsome face continued to appear to her in disturbing dreams – decided to set off down the road that led to the airport and follow through on a plan. It was one of those muggy afternoons before the rainy season, when the khamsin begins to blow and red dust storms appear out of nowhere. While Marianna was sorry to miss a film at the oratory with an actor she liked very much, she would trade some of her figurines for a book, and read instead.

She walked for a long time, the khamsin blowing ever harder. But her many thoughts kept her company; she still kept them hidden away and pulled them out periodically – like lottery tickets – during her long journey.

The house that she was looking for was located near the airport. It was small, white, and had bright green shutters. The gate was green, too, and on it hung a warning sign that said BEWARE OF THE DOG. In fact, as soon as she got close, two large dogs on chains started jumping up and barking wildly, as if the enemy had arrived and they were eager to go to war. Marianna stood staring at the two animals that seemed to want to tear her to shreds, too scared to ring the bell, not wanting to annoy the animals any further. They made so much noise that a large man came to the door. With a single whistled word, the dogs crouched down, started to whimper and stared at him with sad eyes, suddenly transformed into two cowering balls of fur. A cat in the window stretched smugly and looked with disdain at the two dogs.

The large man walked towards the gate.

'What are you doing here, Marianna?' he asked with concern.

'I need to talk to you about something important,' she said quickly, as if the words might slip away before the man could hear them.

'To me?' The carpenter peered at her. 'Is it about Gianfranco?'

'Him, too,' Marianna replied.

He opened the gate. Marianna looked suspiciously at the two dogs. The animals bared their white teeth and growled softly, but when their owner glanced at them, the dogs quieted down and allowed Marianna to enter the house under their protection.

'Have a seat,' the man said, pointing to an armchair near the window. He sat down heavily on the sofa. 'Now, what's the problem?' he asked, fearing some kind of trouble.

Marianna tried to take a deep breath. She had an arduous task in front of her.

'Would you be willing to give your last name to Gianfranco and me?' she asked timidly. 'Just your last name; nothing else.'

'My name?' the man asked, shifting away from her on the sofa.

'Yes,' she said, clenching the fabric of her dress. 'Just your name. And we will never ask you for anything else. You can trust us; our father was Italian.' Marianna knew that the carpenter lived with an Eritrean woman and that they had a daughter.

'*Just* my name,' the carpenter repeated with amazement. He lit a cigarette, inhaled deeply, and then exhaled, causing many small clouds to scatter around the room.

It occurred to Marianna that the carpenter looked a little like the ogre in Tom Thumb, which she had read in an illustrated book that belonged to Signora Antonella, but the carpenter's face was kind. Gianfranco had been working for him for six years and had never complained, even though he had always been paid very little.

'I really need a last name,' Marianna said. 'And so does Gianfranco. With a last name I could go to Italy. I don't want to stay here forever.'

'I see,' the carpenter said, his voice rising in tone, his face starting to turn as red as his hair. 'And you think that I'm going to give you my name, just like that? And then, one day… there will be a problem and who knows what you'll ask me for…'

Marianna got to her feet, offended.

'I said that we would never ask you for anything,' she said firmly. 'And you have to believe me.'

The man looked at her in silence. She had grown into a very pretty girl, elegant even, and she expressed herself very well.

Marianna had the sensation that he was looking at her body, even the parts that were hidden away. She felt her cheeks flush.

'Of course, you wouldn't be able to ask me for anything either,' she said clearly.

The carpenter smiled, showing that he understood what she meant. He glanced once more at her body.

'For you, I'll think about it,' he said. 'But I will definitely not give my last name to Gianfranco. He has worked with me for many years now, I have taught him a skill, and I like him, but I do not want to give him my name. I'd like the relationship between your brother and me to remain professional. Otherwise it would look like…' He stopped and lit another cigarette. 'He'll just have to find someone else.'

Marianna sighed and looked down. She noticed an old teddy bear sitting in a corner, staring off into the distance with its one eye.

'I have a daughter,' the carpenter said. 'And if I ever go back to Italy, I'll bring her and her mother with me.'

Marianna noticed that the carpenter had grown emotional at the thought. She took advantage of the moment. 'I'll find someone else for Gianfranco,' she said. 'But for me, could

I please know your answer now? It won't cost you anything. And I promise that I will never make trouble for you.'

The carpenter felt obliged to believe her. He liked the girl. She was clear-eyed, she had a pleasant smile, and deep dimples on her slender face. From the way Marianna's voice trembled with emotion, it was as if her life depended on the request. Her mother, Sellass, who occasionally stopped by the workshop and always nodded to him courteously, inspired deep respect; she was a proud and strong woman.

'What about your mother?' he asked. 'Doesn't she have a man?'

'My mother has always taken care of us on her own,' Marianna replied proudly. 'She has always worked very hard.'

The carpenter thought about his own daughter. He imagined her, as an adult, having to go to someone she didn't know to ask for a last name, after having lived on her own, abandoned by her father, for so many years. He thought of Gianfranco, the sad and quiet boy who instantly learnt everything he had taught him. Who could say what kind of life that woman and her children would have had if their father had not left them.

'Fine, Marianna,' he said. 'I will give you my name. But remember our pact, understand? I want to believe you.'

'Thank you,' the girl said, her eyes shining brightly. 'And you'll see, I will never give you any trouble. I'll let you know when you have to come and sign the papers. I was told I need two witnesses.'

Escorted by the carpenter, she passed between the two whimpering dogs once more.

She looked at the animals gently, realising that those ferocious guardians wouldn't dare move a whisker. Before walking through the gate, she held out her small hand to shake the carpenter's massive one, to seal their agreement. And then she started to run, joyfully, back to Amba Galliano.

She immediately felt the need to show her gratitude to someone in some way. She would thank God for protecting her; she would thank life for allowing her to exist in its world of light and colours. She had an Italian last name now and, one day, in a distant country, she would have a different life. Her thoughts turned to the little savings she had managed to hide in an envelope under her mattress and then to Padre Lodovico, the old priest at the church in Amba Galliano.

She got home out of breath, grabbed the envelope, and went straight to the church.

Padre Lodovico was sitting in a pew, trying to fix a sandal, which had lost one of its leather straps, but his hands trembled too hard. Marianna quickly made the sign of the cross and walked up to him.

'This is for you, Padre,' she said, handing him the envelope. 'Say some Masses for the dead; I managed to get a last name!' She spoke in such a hurry that the old man was caught off guard.

'But Marianna,' he said softly and slowly, in a voice better suited to that shadowy place. 'You should keep some of this for yourself.'

'No, Padre,' the girl said and firmly set the envelope in his lap. 'I have received a grace from God.'

The old man smiled, his blue eyes shining with childlike wonder and tears.

Marianna sat down next to him.

'Are you tired, Padre?' she asked.

'No,' he replied, shaking his head. 'I am old. And the elderly are fragile, like glass. Do you understand?' He wiped away his tears.

Marianna picked up his sandal and replaced the leather strap.

'You're a good girl,' Padre Lodovico said. He wanted to say more but it was hard for him to talk. 'Let's go,' he said, brushing a fly off his cassock. 'I have many things to do before evening.'

Marianna knelt down and kissed the priest's crucifix. She looked at the altar, with its flickering candles, and the statue of the Virgin Mary, adorned with shiny offerings from the devout, necklaces of gold and silver. She thought of early morning Mass, the scent of incense, the organ music, and the nuns and orphans who regularly lifted their clear voices to the heavens. With all the Masses that she was offering, Marianna thought, the voices of the living would surely reach the distant worlds of the dead and let them know that they were not alone.

37

Sellass had on the dress she wore on Sundays when she went to Mass and then went to greet the people she knew who lived by the church. It was long and white, made of the same fabric as the *zuria* she wore to cover her head, its border decorated with crosses in bright colours. The kohl powder she used to accentuate her large dark eyes sparkled.

She carefully set down a piece of newspaper on the steps outside her house so as not to soil her dress, and then sat down. She looked at the tufts of faded grass and the yellow daisies, their sun-like eyes gazing upon the world with amazement. The pepper tree had grown taller, the maskal with the iridescent feathers still came and sat in its branches, singing amidst its fringed leaves.

Marianna opened the gate, walked through it, and looked at her mother. She seemed unreal, a splendid statue all in white, brought there by a reverie to decorate the garden.

'I've found someone to give me a name,' she said, trying her best to appear calm. 'Gianfranco's boss. Now I have to find two witnesses.'

She gripped her dress and waited anxiously to hear what

Sellass had to say. Her mother continued to look at the tufts of grass, the daisies and the pepper tree. Dusk was approaching; there was the sound of church bells.

'Good,' Sellass said peering intensely at her daughter. 'I hope you don't have to give him anything in exchange for this favour.'

Marianna bit her lip and wished she could scream, she was so offended. She thought of Lina, the girl with the limp who had gone to Signora Antonella's school with her. Marianna had bumped into her a few days before, near the grain market. She was still small and skinny, a little underdeveloped, but she had such a pretty face that people turned to stare at her. She told Marianna that her mother had an incurable illness and now lived with one of their relatives. Lina had not talked about herself at all. Later Marianna had learnt that Lina's mother was an alcoholic and no longer wanted to see her daughter. The girl now lived with an older Italian man, a taxi driver who had been charmed by her beauty and promised to adopt her legally in exchange for her company.

Other girls had also prostituted themselves to obtain a last name that would grant them Italian citizenship, nurturing the hope that one day they could leave the country and find a better life in a place where there wasn't racial prejudice.

'He's an honest man,' Marianna said, annoyed by her mother's comment. 'And I certainly don't need your advice. I know what I need to do.'

'Your brother works twelve-hour days for the man and has never been paid well.'

'Gianfranco has learnt a skill,' Marianna said, trying to defend the carpenter. 'And I don't think he could've found better. Maybe Signor Pino doesn't have that much money.' She glanced at her mother for some sign of approval. 'But he can't give his name to Gianfranco. We'll find someone else for him.'

The corners of Sellass' mouth turned up ever so slightly. Marianna hated it when she smirked like that, as if her mother were making light of important matters.

'Who says that your brother wants an Italian name? He doesn't care about things like that,' Sellass said.

Marianna blushed with embarrassment. It seemed natural to her that Gianfranco would want a name. All the times she had spoken about it with him, he had never said a thing.

She looked at her mother with bitterness and hatred. Sellass had not used the document that their father had left them for anything worthwhile. Maybe their father had left because Sellass was unlovable, maybe she had treated him badly. It occurred to Marianna that her last name ought to be Cinzi. That was her name. Whenever she tried to remember his face and voice, all she could see was a flock of pink flamingos, and then a kite, nothing else.

'As soon as I have enough money saved up, I'm leaving,' she went on to say. She wanted to take advantage of the moment to ask more about her father, to tell Sellass that she wanted to go to Italy to look for him. She recalled what she had seen written down on that piece of paper: his date of birth, the name of the town where he was born. She sighed heavily to hide the fact that she was on the verge of tears. She couldn't speak. She kicked a small rock, bent down and pulled up a handful of grass. A bee flew away in fear.

Sellass stood up and carefully folded the piece of newspaper on which she had been sitting.

'This is your country,' she said softly but emphatically. 'This is your land.'

She continued to stare at Marianna, who felt despair run through her. Her mother wore a cruel expression, as if she was about to beat her, like in their worst moments in Edaga Arbi. Marianna went back to feeling like she did when she was a child, when she used to have to shield herself with her arm for protection, her heart pounding, while Sellass beat her.

She saw her mother's mouth moving, whispering something, but the sound did not reach her. It was as if her lips were forming words but not giving them sound.

Marianna realised that her mother was asking herself the same question she always did: 'How could he...?' and felt her heart fill with deep sorrow. She saw her father vanish like a gust of wind, disappearing into nothing, leaving behind a woman with two small children.

Sellass went inside and closed the door behind her. Marianna sat down heavily on the grass and held her head in her hands.

She thought about Gianfranco. She never really knew what her brother was thinking. It was as if he lived in a different world, one filled with silences that she did not understand. Maybe those silences were a form of escape, like the constant games he played of building and then destroying things. She saw him as a child, with his piles of pebbles, while she kept her ear to the earth, asking for it to transmit the sounds of Sellass' footsteps, back when she still loved her mother. Then she heard Gianfranco arrive home; he had a light step and she recognised it immediately. He sat down next to her on the grass. He picked up a ladybird and put it on his arm. Marianna smiled at him. She looked at his blond hair and green eyes, and thought back to that long-ago day when Elsa had looked at him with wonder. He was so handsome and sombre that sometimes it hurt to look at him. She often wondered why the carpenter had never adopted this extraordinary boy.

They sat together for some time before she asked him the question.

'Are you interested in having a last name?'

He watched the ladybird fly off, then picked a blade of grass and put it in his mouth. Marianna looked at his nails, chewed down to the quick, his hands scarred by minor accidents at work.

'No,' Gianfranco said. 'I don't care about that.'

Marianna needed to change the subject as she felt like she was going to cry. 'Do you remember how many chameleons we used to find when we were little?'

Gianfranco smiled. 'We could never keep them for long. Maybe they found their way home, back to the woods.'

Then he stood up and went to his work table in the corner, where he built and took apart his contraptions, over and over.

38

Marianna placed her few belongings in a bag, then looked around her slowly. She had dreamt of living in a house like the one in Amba Galliano for a very long time. A house with no holes in the roof and with lots of windows, so the sun could shine in. Even Zubuc had known that one day they would manage to buy a home; his branches always quivered whenever Marianna talked about the beautiful place where they would one day live. And now here she was leaving Amba Galliano, the pepper tree, the maskal that had sung there for years, its feathers changing from grey to the colour of the setting sun.

Marianna knew everything about the house: its silences, the chirring of insect wings, the melodious sound of women passing by their gate, the way the wind rustled through the leaves of the pepper tree. She knew the tolling of the bells at the small church where she went each Sunday to help serve Mass, the squeak of the gate, she recognised the food vendors from their footsteps and the way they called out their wares. She knew so much about that house that, at times, she felt at one with it, she recognised its presence and spirit, she could hear it breathing during the night, in the dark, when everything else was silent.

And now she was leaving her mother, brother and the house to go and live in the pension at the Comboni mission run by the nuns. She could not stay with her mother anymore; between them was only silence and bitterness.

Marianna looked at the painting of the Virgin Mary, a black Madonna with a wistful expression and blue mantle, faded with time. She wondered what prayers Sellass had said to the sad Mary who had always been with them.

She heard her mother at the front door.

'I'm leaving,' Marianna said as Sellass walked in.

'I know,' Sellass said, without moving. She did not take off her futah, she did not put down her zembil. Her face looked weary and she had dark circles under her eyes, but she was still a great beauty.

'I can't stay here any longer,' Marianna added. 'Suor Eleonora told me that there's a free bed at the Comboni mission.' She looked at her mother boldly, worried she might reply cruelly.

Sellass just stood in the doorway, staring at her daughter without saying a word.

'Tomorrow I will stop by Signor Pino's workshop to say goodbye to Gianfranco,' Marianna said, taking two handkerchiefs out of a box, then folding them up and placing them in her purse.

Sellass could smell the scent of low tide, she heard the call of a seagull. Carlo was watching her as she carefully folded her own clothes and those of the children, placing them in a sack. They would take the bus to Adi Ugri. He would stay behind. He continued to watch her, his blue eyes following her every move in the house at the salt flats. She was leaving. She would never see him again.

'As soon as I can, I'm going to Italy,' Marianna said to Sellass, waiting for her mother's reaction, hoping her words had reminded her of her father.

'To Italy...' Sellass said so softly that only she could hear the words. She sighed, took off her futah, and put down her zembil.

Marianna picked up her bag and left. After closing the gate behind her, she turned around to look one last time at the house, to see if her mother had come to the door. But Sellass was not there. All the lights were off. As she walked towards the mission, she thought of all the terrible times in Edaga Arbi when Sellass had hit her; she told herself that she was doing the right thing, that Sellass did not love her. She tried to erase everything from her mind: thoughts of her mother, Gianfranco, Amba Galliano. She tried to only see her future, a different country. Maybe one day she would meet her father and comprehend why he had abandoned them, maybe his love for them had never waned, maybe there had been a misunderstanding that had led to him being separated from them.

Marianna ran all the way to the Comboni mission and arrived there out of breath. She rang the bell. Ines, a mixed-race servant her own age, opened the door and accompanied her to a room with two beds. Sitting on one of them was Rita, another mixed-race girl around the same age, trimming her fingernails.

'Hello,' she said, putting her scissors down on the bed. 'There's room for your things in the closet. I won't be here for very long.' She crossed her long legs and went back to her nails. She was stunning: tall and shapely, with beautiful curly hair and large brown eyes. Marianna had heard about her but they had never spent any time together. She knew that Rita had grown up with the nuns and that once she ran away, causing quite a stir. They had found her two days later on the road that led to Massawa. Rita was courted by a great many men, especially older European ones, and the nuns saw her great beauty as a perpetual threat to the harmony of the boarding house. The girl was both cunning and kind, and since she gave them no proof of her vocation towards a life of sin, she always managed to reassure the nuns and banish their fears.

'You're leaving?' Marianna stared at her with curiosity, noticing that she was wearing a pretty dress and beautiful shoes with a bit of a heel.

'I'm fed up with the nuns,' Rita said, putting down her scissors again. 'I'm fed up with this life, with always having to invent stories, going to Mass every single morning; with all the money I've collected for the dead, I've earned myself a place in heaven for sure.'

She then went on to confide in Marianna that she was in love with a married man, a well-known businessman.

'He's much older than me,' she said. 'For some reason – probably because of my father, the English colonel – I always seem to fall in love with older men... Anyway, one day soon he'll leave his wife and we'll live together, but for now I'm going to go live in an apartment in the centre of town.' She ran a hand through her curly locks.

Marianna thought about Gilberto; maybe he had tried to court Rita, too.

'He promised that he'd take me with him to Italy,' Rita added. 'He said we'll go all sorts of pretty places, and that he'll introduce me to people in the world of cinema.'

'Do you want to become an actress?' Marianna asked with surprise, but at the same time she realised that Rita could truly pull it off; she was beautiful and clearly knew how to act. She could see her in a long tight dress, her generous lips painted bright red, draped in bracelets and necklaces, surrounded by journalists and photographers. The little mulatto orphan who goes on to become a world-famous actress; the story would be in all the newspapers. Maybe they'd even make figurines based on her, Marianna thought, like the ones of Ava Gardner that they gave away with ice cream cones.

A bell rang, loud and long, announcing that dinner was ready. Suor Eleonora peered into the room to confirm that Marianna had arrived. Then she noticed Rita's long, bare legs and sighed, reaching for her crucifix. 'You need to lower the hem of your dress, young lady,' she said.

'It's funny, but I seem to keep growing,' the girl replied with a smile. 'My father must have been English.'

Rita often spoke about how her hypothetical English father – probably a colonel, tall and distinct, surely from an aristocratic family – had fallen in love with an Eritrean woman and then been forced to leave the country, causing her mother to die of heartbreak, and leaving her daughter on her own.

Suor Eleonora pretended not to hear her. 'As for you,' she said, looking at Marianna. 'Punctuality and tidiness are key. Do your best to get along with everyone.'

Ines showed Marianna to her seat in the dimly lit dining room. Sitting on a bench next to the window were three little mixed-race girls. They wore blue pinafores and all three had their hair tied back with ribbons.

'Who are they?' Marianna asked, feeling a deep sadness rise up inside her, the dark shadow of loneliness and anxiety.

'Three orphans,' Ines said. 'They're all the same age, three years old. Two of them were abandoned shortly after birth, I don't think their mothers could afford to keep them. The other one, Teresa, has only been here a little while.' She bent down and whispered in Marianna's ear. 'Her mother lived with an Italian man who was terribly jealous. He killed her, stabbed her with a knife, right in front of the child. You probably heard the story: the mechanic on Corso del Re?'

Marianna nodded.

'Hurry up, Ines,' Suor Eleonora's measured voice resonated through the room.

Marianna sat down next to an elderly lady who had been living in the pension for many years. She was sad and silent, as if she found herself among the living purely by mistake. Her skin was pale and waxen, and her thin hair was a faded whitish-yellow.

Marianna continued to stare at the little girls. One of them whispered something to the others, after which they stood up, made their way to a table, and began to eat their soup, dripping some onto their napkins and picking out the pieces of bread with their hands. At the end of the meal, they stood up in unison and looked around the room. They moved as if following a familiar ritual.

Marianna tried to wave them over, but the little girls looked straight through her, as if she were air, and then walked out of the room in utter silence.

'What good little girls,' Marianna said to Ines, who was clearing the tables. 'And so quiet.'

Ines shrugged. 'They live in their own world. No one has time for them. People here are always so busy. They get by, they're always together and they don't talk much. One of them doesn't even speak, little Teresa stutters, and all three of them still wet their beds at night.'

The elderly lady at Marianna's table got to her feet, looked kindly around the room, as if leaving a place that she had loved a great deal, nodded, and walked out.

Marianna made her way over to the window and stared outside.

The darkness was deep. Long shadows hinted at the presence of trees and flowerbeds. A dog barked in the distance, other dogs started to bark excitedly in reply. The stars peered down on the darkness like bright eyes. Marianna wanted to cry. She felt far away from everything, exiled from the world, as if she were on one of those stars, disappearing into nothingness.

39

Elsa, Tedla and Ras, the stray dog, sat together in a sunny spot, keeping each other company. Elsa said something and laughed, her face breaking into small wrinkles, her eyes shining brightly. Tedla nodded. He wore a long white tunic and his beard and hair were dotted with flowers and butterflies, creating an image of great beauty. All of the sores that Ras once had were gone, and his fur shone in the sunlight; he chewed on a bone, looking up every so often at the two elderly people. The sand was white and shone brightly. Birds flew overhead with their wings spread wide, cawing and then disappearing, but their shadows remained behind, imprinted on the white sand. Their shadows were easy to see.

High up in a palm tree was a kite with blue eyes. It stared down at the two old people and the dog. Its fringed tail blew this way and that in the wind.

Elsa picked a daisy out of the air and started removing its petals one by one, whispering some words as she did so. Tedla imitated Elsa, his hands moving lightly through the air, as if he, too, were picking off daisy petals.

'What did you say?' Elsa asked, leaning closer to Tedla so he could whisper into her ear. The old man smiled as if he had an important secret.

'Dreams,' he said softly. 'Yes, no, yes, no. Which one counts, the first or the last?'

'Was it Edaga Arbi?' Elsa asked. 'Or the cemetery at night? Or Marianna?' She paused for a moment. 'Or was it the wind?'

'I don't know if the first one counts or the last one,' the old man said, shaking his head. 'Or was it the sparks?'

A poor woman came crawling towards them on her hands, dragging her twisted legs behind her. Her head and shoulders were covered by a futah and she wore large gold hoops in her ears.

Pulling herself along with the help of tin cans made her journey faster and less tiresome. She stopped next to the two elderly people and greeted them. It appeared that they knew each other well. Then she took a small pouch out of her dress, unknotted it and let the shells fall to the sand. They formed the shape of a star. The shadows of birds on the beach, their wings spread open wide, kept increasing.

'And that means...?' Elsa asked impatiently, looking from one shell to the next.

'Does the first one count or the last?' Tedla asked again, batting at the air.

The woman with the shells shrugged. She looked around and took a deep breath. There was so much light and so many colours. The kite whispered something to them with its vermilion mouth.

'Maybe it's magic,' the elderly woman said, waiting for a nod of agreement from Elsa and Tedla. 'It could well be...' she said again, stroking the shells with a finger.

'I believe it is,' Elsa said, sighing deeply. 'It was all so colourful.'

'Does magic have a colour?' Tedla asked, his hands coming to rest in his lap. The women had to ask him to repeat himself several times because he spoke so softly.

'It is life,' the kite whispered from up above. 'Life is magic,' it said, closing its eyes and exhaling, its breath transforming into a bird that flew away, leaving its shadow on the sand. And then all the hues melded together into a single shape: a large bell with blue eyes and vermilion lips that tolled the hours, with each knelled hour rising into the air in the form of a cloud.

It rang six times. Marianna awoke with the figures from her dream in her mind's eye. She tried to preserve them for as long as possible, before the day made them disappear: she pulled her blanket over her head, curled up, and tried to go back to sleep, to return to the dream, but it had already vanished with the tolling bell. Marianna got out of bed. She could hear the sound of the nuns and maids getting ready for the day, and the birds outside were chirping eagerly.

There was great excitement that morning at the Giubelli sisters' workshop. Marianna swiftly basted a slip for a dress, while frequently glancing at the clock on the wall. At twelve o'clock there would be a solar eclipse. People had been discussing it for days, the tension in the air was palpable. This was an important event that people would talk about for a long time to come. Finally, the time came, everyone rushed outside into the courtyard and found a patch of grass where they could sit and watch the sky.

Marianna stared with great emotion as the great star gradually darkened. The sisters held up a special piece of glass that allowed them to see the eclipse even better. Their elderly maid, Abeba, crossed herself and fearfully said her prayers. The vendors and beggars stopped and looked up at the sky in wonder. They were amazed and scared: it was a dark omen, indeed, if the sun they knew so well wanted to hide something terribly sad under the dark shadow that was slowly covering it.

Marianna got to her feet and went to the gate; she had heard a cry of pain from under the palm tree.

The crippled woman who dragged herself through the streets of Asmara was praying for something or someone. A little boy rushed over to her and held her hand tightly.

Marianna was very disturbed by the eclipse. She thought back to the days in Edaga Arbi when she used to sit in the courtyard, waiting for the sun to climb into the sky so that she could go and buy injera, how she bowed deeply to her bright friend in order to feel loved. No one could explain this solar event to her, not even Suor Eleonora could tell her why the sun would go dark. Padre Gabriele would've been able to explain it, Marianna thought. He would have been able to reveal the mystery to her.

Slowly, the sun became a darkened disc, the world went quiet, and even the birds stopped singing in the trees. Everything was enveloped in shadows, the heat had disappeared, it was as if a magic spell had been cast over the world. The crippled woman turned towards Marianna. Her face was ageless, her dark eyes filled with grief.

'Bad times lie ahead for our people,' she said, breaking the silence. 'Soon this country will become as dark as the sun.'

An old beggar bent down and repeatedly kissed the earth, invoking God. A blind man raised his spent eyes towards the sky and then, shivering with cold, pulled his rags tightly around him. The little boy sitting beside him lifted a canister of water to the elderly man's dry lips.

Marianna went back and sat down next to the two sisters. Anna handed her the darkened glass so that she could see the eclipse better. Then, slowly, the sun went back to shining. For the rest of the day no one spoke of anything else. Marianna checked on the sun now and then, just to make sure that it was the same bright star it had always been. To her mind, the eclipse had been the sun's moment of sadness, of grief. She couldn't help but think of the crippled woman, her look of concern, and her words, which truly frightened Marianna.

'I have to leave,' she thought. 'I have to leave this country.'

It was Abramo, the Jewish man who owned a shop on Corso del Re, who explained the phenomenon of the eclipse to Marianna. She had gone to his haberdashery to buy buttons. Abramo, who liked Marianna, kept her longer than necessary by talking about it at length. A heavyset and good-natured man, Abramo spoke a number of languages so convincingly that no one ever knew which was his native tongue. His shop was filled from floor to ceiling with fabric, buttons, trimmings and drapes, all of which seemed to be piled up randomly, but he knew where to find exactly what his clients wanted in an instant and, without ever laying it on too thick, he knew how to sing the praises of even an old spool of thread. He was in his shop from morning until night, and after they closed up, he stood behind the counter, counting how much money he had made and jotting down notes. A young, reserved, mixed-race girl with a sweet but timid smile helped him serve the clients and tried to tidy up the shelves.

When Marianna came into the shop, the young girl gave her the buttons she needed, but Abramo gestured to her to wait. He was busy serving a client, a distinguished Italian lady, who was having difficulty finding just the right fabric for some curtains. Marianna observed the woman closely but discreetly, with both curiosity and admiration. She was in awe of her long golden hair, her large turquoise eyes, her pretty green dress. She also liked the sound of her voice and the way she had painted her lips pink. As the lady was leaving, after agreeing on curtains that Abramo had pulled out as if they were the only ones suitable for her, the woman smiled offhandedly at Marianna. She left behind a trail of flowery perfume.

'What elegance,' Abramo commented, rolling up the bolts of fabric. It seemed to Marianna that he, too, was revelling in the lady's fragrance. And then, in the few moments they had alone, he explained the eclipse to her, and also hinted at the vastness of the universe with its millions of stars.

'Marianna,' Abramo said suddenly, interrupting his explanation of the moon, as if struck by a sudden thought. 'My wife and I recently opened a shop in Addis Ababa. She is already there, starting up the business, and soon I will join her. We need a capable girl to help us – why don't you come and work with us?' While waiting for Marianna to answer, he noted her pleasant appearance and natural elegance.

Marianna rested her packet of buttons on the counter. In those few seconds she thought of many things all at once, and with some confusion.

'We'll pay you well,' Abramo added. 'The shop will be magnificent, much larger than this one. Addis is a busy city, full of people and movement, and all the embassies are there.'

Marianna thought about Italy. If she were to move to Addis with the Menahem family, she would be one step closer to making her dream come true. The fact that this opportunity had suddenly presented itself to her seemed almost too good to be true. She could leave, move to a different city, lead a new life, meet new people; the Menahems had always been kind to her and she already liked them very much.

'What do you say?' Abramo asked, placing a hand on her shoulder. 'You don't want to stay here forever, sewing hems. You don't want to marry the first man you meet. You're an intelligent girl, Marianna, and you should aspire to something greater. By seeing the world a little, you will grow. And you'll be happy with us.' He pointed to the other girl, who was standing nearby, organising buttons. 'She's coming with us, too,' he added.

Marianna smiled widely, her face filling with light.

'When?' she asked softly.

'We'll let you know,' Abramo said. 'In the meantime, tell your mother, the nuns and the Giubelli sisters.'

Marianna left the shop feeling as light as a cloud. The sun was rapidly setting, birds flew noisily overhead, they had already forgotten about the exceptional events of the day.

The Corso was crowded with people out for their evening stroll, content to meet up in their usual places on the palm-lined street, to chat with their friends and see that nothing and no one had changed. It was a form of validation, that slow evening walk, a confirmation of their own protected existence in that sunny corner of the world.

Marianna strode quickly up the street, then ran to the Comboni mission. For her, Asmara was a place that she needed to escape from as quickly as possible. It felt like the mountains that ringed the city were closing in on her, restricting her space a little more every day. Soon she would have no air left to breathe.

She thought of Rita and how she had said she would be leaving the Comboni mission. She had tipped back her head and laughed, but Marianna had seen a flash of sadness in her dark eyes.

'You're all the same,' Suor Claudia had said to them some evenings earlier. 'Good-for-nothings, wastrels.'

Marianna's eyes stung with tears. She had so many confused thoughts and images: Gianfranco, Sellass, the Giubelli sisters, the nuns. She saw a bright, spacious shop in Addis Ababa with splendid merchandise and crowds of people of all races making their purchases. She saw herself: beautiful, smiling, gliding between ladies in elegant necklaces and soft silks. And then she saw Italy, her dream finally coming true.

40

Sellass sat in a corner of the courtyard, flinging the chicken's mottled feathers this way and that. Zegai, chewing on a piece of bark, watched as the soft plumage flew through the air, catching the light. The dog eyed the bird with the floppy neck. Sellass plucked the feathers forcefully, as if each one was a concern that she was trying to cast to the wind.

When the bird was nothing more than a glassy-eyed carcass covered with black dots where the feathers had been, Zegai sighed and started to tidy up. Some of the plumage had blown a little distance away and settled into the pattern of a wing, as if longing for the life lost.

Zegai hesitated momentarily, then bent down to gather them up.

He was used to sudden explosions of wrath from Sellass. She never shouted or used bad words like Signora Giustina did. No, Sellass either threw feathers, aggressively emptied out buckets of water, or shook pillows and slapped rugs so violently it felt like the house might break.

Zegai placed the feathers in a paper bag and walked past Sellass, grumbling to himself, but softly, so as not to anger her any further. Just then, Marianna appeared at the gate and called to her mother. Zegai nodded at her in greeting and she smiled at him.

'I need to talk to you,' Marianna said to her mother.

Sellass washed her hands at a faucet in the courtyard, disappeared into the room she used for changing and came out a few moments later.

She had removed her apron and picked up her futah, which she wrapped around her shoulders and over her head. She said something to Zegai and made her way towards the gate. From an upstairs window, Giustina saw the two women walk away. She had witnessed the flight of feathers and was aware that Sellass could have easily placed them in the basket by her side and not wasted Zegai's time, but she had not dared say anything. Over the years, she had come to realise just how precious Sellass was and, even if she scolded her occasionally, she did not want to risk offending her; a great number of other families would have been thrilled to have her. One evening she had seen the two children, Gianfranco and Marianna, at the gate; they had brought their mother a key. That was the day she had seen with her own eyes that they were mulatto; her friends had mentioned the rumours to her. Despite not being terribly interested in Sellass' life, Giustina was curious to know more about the man who had left them, but when she tried to ask about him, Sellass had only stared coldly back at her. Why are you asking me about it now, her haughty look seemed to say, after so many years of not caring.

Not long after, Giustina had seen the children again, near the cathedral, and she was stunned by their beauty. For a moment she considered all the years that Sellass had managed to work and take care of them – when had she had the time? – and came to the conclusion that it really was none of her business and that she ought not get involved in those matters. Many children in Asmara had been abandoned by their Italian fathers. They could be seen roaming the streets, living in religious institutes and missions, somehow they managed to grow up. And for those with an Italian name, well, the Consulate was trying to do something for them, Giustina told herself. Even so, she continued to think about the boy with the golden hair, about the sad and distant look in his eyes, as if he was suffering in exile from the rest of the world, and about Marianna's luminous smile. She watched the two young women walk down the street and stepped away from the window.

'What's the matter?' Sellass asked, covering the lower part of her face. She always spoke to her children in Tigrinya.

'I'm leaving,' Marianna said, smoothing down her dress. 'I've already told the nuns and the Giubelli sisters. I'm moving to Addis Ababa with the Menahems. They've offered me a job in their new shop.' She glanced at her mother to see what the effect of her words might be, but there was none. Sellass merely stared at a spot in the distance.

The silence was oppressive. Marianna tried to find words to break the unease. 'They're good people, and I'll be able to save up some money. Then I'll go to Italy. I want to leave.'

Sellass stopped, leant against the wall of an old house and looked at her daughter.

'Good,' she murmured. 'If that's what you want… to go to…' She couldn't finish the sentence, her final word became just a breath.

'I don't want to stay here, in this country,' Marianna said.

'But it's your country,' Sellass said in a whisper.

Marianna clutched her skirt in her fist. 'No,' she said calmly. 'It is not my country. I want to go to Italy.' She looked down at her mother's bare feet. She realised that Sellass had never worn a pair of shoes, not even now that plastic sandals were inexpensive, and yet it looked like she had always walked on carpets: her feet, painted red with henna, were smooth and slender.

'I'm sad to leave Gianfranco behind,' she added. 'And I hope that one day he'll come to Italy too.'

'No,' Sellass said with a sigh. 'He'll stay here. He is not like you.'

The church bells tolled slowly and sadly, announcing a funeral Mass.

'He needs to leave this country,' Marianna said.

Sellass felt her chest tighten with despair. For a brief moment, Marianna had reminded her of Mariam. There had been a flash of light in her eyes or maybe it was the intonation of her voice; something had briefly taken Sellass back to the spot where Mariam had spent her days. She could smell the scent of Mariam's clothes, infused with the odours and aromas of life in Massawa. Then, as if it had only been a few seconds ago, she visualised the children with the multicoloured pebbles, and Mariam's shells on the ground, and Ahmed's somewhat foggy gaze.

Then she saw the boulders where she went to greet the wind, she heard footsteps approaching, and even before she could turn around to look, she saw those eyes, eyes the colour of the sea. And when she bent down again and asked the crippled woman to throw the shells and read her future, Mariam sighed, as if carrying a heavy burden. The Sellass of those days, who used to walk up and down the streets singing, seemed like another person entirely. Maybe the girl who had wanted to know her destiny had not been her. That image of herself, like a daughter she had loved and soon lost, returned to her every so often, reawakening an ancient sorrow.

Then the moment vanished, taking her memories with it, and Sellass could no longer see the glimmering light that had led her back to Mariam.

A bird sang in the branches of a jacaranda tree, causing its bluish flowers to flutter to the ground, and the tolling bell slowly faded.

'I have to go back now,' Sellass said.

Marianna noticed that something had upset her mother. She could tell by the way her breath came up short. A sudden gust of wind showered them with jacaranda flowers. Marianna watched as they landed on Sellass' shoulders and her bare feet. She thought back to Edaga Arbi and all the times her mother had hit her: she would never be able to love her mother. All those times she had reached out to touch her just to make sure she was real, they were but a distant memory.

'*Ci vedremo*,' Marianna said in Italian. 'I'll come and say goodbye before I leave.'

That evening, Sellass found Gianfranco sitting outside the house in the dark, immobile, absorbed in his thoughts. Sellass sat down quietly on the step next to him. A firefly rose up into the sky, its tiny lantern dancing in the darkness. Then other fireflies arrived. It was as if many small eyes had lit up the air and wandered through it, trying to follow the exhalations of the earth. Gianfranco watched the little lights carefully.

'Your sister is leaving,' Sellass whispered, moving closer to him. She wished she could talk to him but she knew that her son's existence was built on silence. Ever since he was little, he had spent hours immersed in his thoughts or in an imaginary world. It occurred to her that he had been helping the carpenter make coffins since he was a child, he had always gone to work on time, and sometimes he had even worked through the night. Sellass was weary, her thoughts were confused, her eyelids felt heavy. She saw the dead people who would be entrusted to the earth in their wooden coffins, she saw them leave their dark boxes transformed, as if they were clouds, and travel to that distant world where souls chanted sadly in unison. When she was a child, back in her village, her aunt Alefesc had told her that in the deep of night, when even the earth held its breath, you could hear that melancholy chant hum through the air, resonating between the bright stars. It was not the universe that sang when it felt alone, but the souls who resided in it.

Gianfranco rested his hand on his mother's shoulder. 'Mama,' he whispered. 'You're tired. Go to bed.'

She sat up with a jolt and looked around. From a faraway village came the muffled sound of tambourines. The fireflies were gone.

41

Signor Prandi sat down heavily on the sofa. He had dark circles under his eyes and was visibly upset. His wife ran her hand through her silvery hair, as if trying to ease the pain, then took a portrait of their daughters, who had been living in Italy for years, and placed it in the suitcase.

Sellass quietly folded and packed up articles of clothing. She carefully wrapped the knick-knacks that were so dear to Signora Giustina. She thought about how Marianna had stood anxiously before her and predicted that they would need to leave the country, that something bad would happen.

Almost twenty years had passed since that day, but Sellass remembered her daughter as if she had just left; she saw the jacaranda flowers fluttering down on her pink skirt, she recalled how her long braid had been tied with an old ribbon, how her voice had trembled when she spoke of her decision. She remembered her gaze, always so deeply piercing, how much her eyes resembled his. 'How could he...?' Sellass surprised herself by mumbling, as if she had no control over the words, as if the question had never died, never left her. She thought of Padre Gabriele. For years, he had been living at a mission in the heartland of Ethiopia. Whenever he came to Asmara, he brought her Marianna's greetings and read her the letters that she had written him. After living in Addis Ababa for a few years, Marianna had moved to Italy where she found a job, got married, and resumed her studies.

After the carpenter returned to his homeland, Gianfranco went to work in Saudi Arabia. Sellass knew that life there was hard, but Gianfranco had been well paid and eager to save up some money, because Asmara had little to offer. The forced annexation of Eritrea by Ethiopia had led to the beginning of a long civil war, the country had grown poor, and many Europeans had decided to return home.

Guerrilla warriors had recently entered the city in an attempt to take it over. There was the frequent sound of gunshots, Ethiopian soldiers broke into houses and massacred entire families, the wounded were taken to the cathedral, which had been converted into a hospital. Only at night, after curfew, was there silence, together with an oppressive calm. The great clock tower, which continued to toll, measured out an era of death.

An airlift had been arranged for the few Italians who remained. All foreigners needed to be evacuated immediately. People rushed about, they could only take small bags, they had to leave behind both belongings and memories.

'We must leave now,' Giustina said, entering the room where Sellass was packing her bags. 'We can't take anything else.'

Sellass sighed and continued to fold the Signora's light sweaters. She thought back to when she had wished the whites would leave her country. Now that the moment had come, she felt only deep sorrow. There was war, fear and desperation; the Ethiopians were confiscating everything, and Eritreans continued to die. It had been going on for twenty years.

That very morning, she had seen Zegai – on his way to meet up with his wife and mother in Arbaroba, his children had been at the front for years – get shot down in the street, his chest ripped open. She had run to him, hoping he was still alive, but all she could do was close his glassy eyes and say a prayer for him.

The cat came into the room and leapt up onto the bed. Its yellow eyes, misty with age, suspiciously observed Sellass' every move; its tail was stiff with tension.

'I have no idea what you packed,' Giustina said, 'but I trust you. I can't do a thing, I can't even think straight.'

A car horn sounded in the street. Giustina stood up, attempted to fix her hair, and put on her overcoat. She then walked towards Sellass and stopped in front of her. She looked at her face, still so beautiful and proud, her dark eyes outlined in kohl, hiding all her emotion. In that moment, Sellass was Asmara, home, the life she had led in Africa. She wished she could bring her with her, and have her reassuring presence close by, wherever she went.

'Are you sure you won't join us in Italy, Sellass?'

Sellass shook her head.

'But your daughter is there,' Giustina added.

'I will die in my own country,' Sellass said, bending down to close the suitcase. The car horn sounded again. Signor Prandi came into the room and squeezed both of Sellass' hands very tightly.

'Farewell, Sellass,' he said, his voice breaking with emotion. 'Thank you for everything.'

They hurried downstairs and made their way towards the automobile.

'Farewell Signor, farewell Signora,' Sellass stood immobile at the front gate. '*Buona fortuna*. Send my greetings to your daughters. Say hello to Carla.' A vein in her neck pulsed, her hands, crossed over her belly, trembled slightly.

The dog barked frantically, howled, and jumped around, trying to get free of its long chain. The Prandis did their best not to look and climbed into the car. Sellass saw them turn back towards her, Signora Giustina's eyes were filled with tears.

Sellass returned indoors. The cuckoo clock sounded the hour, as if nothing had changed and life would go on as always. Everything was in perfect order, there was not a speck of dust anywhere. The porcelain ballerinas raised their arms up high, the wise old ivory men stared off into the distance, a rose was slowly dying in a small vase.

Sellass ran her hand over Carla's piano, which she had dusted every day for years, every so often tapping one of the keys. She went into the girls' room. Old teddy bears, eyes missing, lay on the beds as if waiting for their owners to return.

When evening and its shadows arrived, Sellass closed all the shutters and lit a candle. She looked out into the street, but no one was there. It was as if life had gone far away and taken all sounds with it. Even the leaves on the trees seemed to be made of glass. The following day, after taking the cat and dog to a friend of the Prandis', she would leave, Sellass thought to herself.

She put out the candle and lay down on the carpet. On that last night in the house, she would sleep in their living room, with all its knick-knacks and paintings of the sea and flowers.

Images from days gone by, imprisoned by time within those four walls, returned to her in the dark, as if on a stage, bringing a variety of scenes and sounds from the past to life.

ND# 42

Sellass stopped in front of the house in Amba Galliano and looked at the two soldiers sitting on the steps where Gianfranco used to sit in the dark, his thoughts wandering like the fireflies he watched.

'*Cuhum?*' one of the soldiers shouted at her. He stood up and walked towards the gate, spitting bitterly on the ground. He held his bayonet in one hand and rested the other hand on a gun attached to his belt. He was young, just a teenager; his eyes were yellow, as if he were unwell, and his hands shook.

'What do you want?' the soldier shouted again.

'This used to be my house,' Sellass said softly but articulating the words carefully to let him know that she would stand there as long as she wanted and without the least bit of fear.

The pepper tree had been cut down, the earth around the base of the plant where the maskal had once sung was all dug up; from the way the walls of the house were blackened with smoke, Sellass presumed that the soldiers had used the trunk and branches to build a fire.

When Gianfranco left for Saudi Arabia, she moved into the Prandis' house and rented out her own house to a kind and well-educated Eritrean man with a good reputation. But after the man disappeared – he may have been among the corpses left in the main square, strangled with wire – the Ethiopians confiscated her house. Sellass stared at the two men. Now both of them stood before her, on the other side of the gate, their eyes filled with hatred and surprise.

'You have to leave,' the older of the two said calmly. 'You're not allowed to stand there. This is not your house anymore.'

Sellass looked them up and down carefully, as if trying to understand who these *tor sarauit* were, what kind of people went around killing and burning down houses. She was not afraid. She was filled with infinite silence and emptiness, and felt no emotion. She was entirely alone, as if the world had become a desert, and the only figures moving around were the shades of the dead, miming the story of the living.

She glanced one last time at the house. Then, after glaring into the eyes of the soldiers as if to tell them how small, ridiculous and unimportant they were, she turned around and walked back to town, pulling her futah tightly around her. At that early hour of the day, the fabric still smelt clean and fresh.

For a brief moment she thought she saw the cart and driver that had brought her few belongings to the house in Amba Galliano one early morning long ago. She recalled how the sunshine had filled the rooms as the children walked through them in amazement.

Walking swiftly – her pace had not changed with the passing years – she crossed the city. Only soldiers were out; people were afraid of leaving their homes, there had been too many killings. Ambulances and trucks passed by. In the distance there was the rhythmic sound of gunfire.

Sellass walked close to the walls and kept her face covered. She carried a large zembil containing a few belongings.

She arrived at the grain market. Gone were the old merchants who called out their wares in loud voices. She saw overturned crates and animal carcasses; the odour of death and spices hung in the air.

Then Sellass saw Haile, the young jujube vendor. He was crying and trying to gather up all the dried fruit that had scattered every which way. Only a few years old, his zembil was larger than he was. His torn shirt was the colour of dust and barely covered his slightly distended belly. He had the chubby cheeks of a little black angel and large beautiful eyes. When the child caught sight of Sellass, he tried to stop crying and wiped his face with his dirty hand but then his breath caught in his throat and he started sobbing again, while running after a berry that had rolled towards the carcass of a horse.

'What are you doing here?' Sellass asked gently, going up to the child. 'Can't you see that no one is out, only soldiers? Who are you going to sell your jujubes to?'

Haile looked up at her and seemed to relax. He wiped away his tears.

'You have to go home,' Sellass added. 'There's a war going on. Can't you hear the guns?'

The little one started to cry again. 'A tor sarauit took some jujubes and knocked the rest over,' he said. Then he pointed in the direction of Edaga Arbi. 'There's no one left up there. My grandmother and brothers are all gone. I don't know where they are. No one is there.'

Sellass squeezed her lips firmly together. She wished she could sit down near the empty crates, let the child rest his head in her lap, and never move again.

'I have to sell my jujubes,' Haile sobbed.

'Let's go,' Sellass said. 'I'm on my way to Edaga Arbi. There must be someone you can stay with until your family returns.'

The little boy walked alongside her, forgetting about the fallen fruit. He seemed calmer and walked quickly, sometimes running, to keep up with her, dragging his zembil behind.

Dark, heavy clouds filled the sky. It started to rain lightly, there was the pungent odour of wet earth, and then it stopped, as if a cloud had toyed with them before being blown away.

Once they reached Edaga Arbi, Sellass stopped in front of a dilapidated house and knocked on the flimsy window. A toothless old woman with bristly tufts of white hair appeared at the door.

'Is it safe to go further?' Sellass asked, after greeting her and embracing her in the customary manner.

The woman nodded and looked at the child.

Sellass pulled some paper bills out of her dress and handed them to the woman. 'Tell your daughter to take care of this child,' she said. 'He is the same age as her own. And then try and find out where his grandmother and brothers are.'

The old woman took a deep breath, her large chest expanding, and sighed heavily, invoking the name of the Virgin Mary, and looking at the little one. She rested a hand on his head. 'These are hard times,' she said, 'but we'll take care of him, don't worry.' Then, lowering her voice, she went on. 'They came around here, too. A lot of people ran off, many were killed. They even killed a poor mute girl, a strange but beautiful child. They took her to the lake, she struggled to get free, but no one could help her.'

'I know who that is,' Haile said. 'I used to see her walking around. She was always quiet. A bird stole her voice. I used to give her some of my jujubes.'

Sellass looked at the old woman, nodded farewell, then made her way to the shack where she had lived for years. She pushed aside the old tin gate, went into the room and looked around. There were no doors, the floor was covered with red dust, a few pieces of burnt wood lay in a heap.

Sellass pulled a mat out of her zembil, unrolled it and sat down in the courtyard near where Zubuc and his little singing friends used to be.

Dark clouds filled the sky, followed by rays of bright sunshine. Sellass wiped her face with a handkerchief, then took an envelope out of her zembil. She removed a piece of paper, yellow with age, unfolded it and stared at the letters written on it for some time. To her eyes, they were just dark spots. Some of them reminded her of bird wings. She returned to that long-ago morning when Carlo had written down that Marianna and Gianfranco were his children and that they could have his last name. Two other men had signed the paper and then Carlo had handed her the envelope. This was the document that Marianna had been looking for; she remembered when Padre Gabriele had asked her about it. But Carlo had left them, and so everything about him had to disappear. It was only right that his children never learn his name.

Sellass could practically feel the heat, taste the salt, hear the muffled sound of the sea. She looked at the paper again, eyes clouded with tears. The small signs blurred together. Slowly, she tore the note into small pieces and dug a hole in the ground where Zubuc had once lived. Then, as if burying a memory that refused to disappear, she gently piled some earth on top of the scraps of paper and patted it all down gently, making it smooth and compact.

Sighing heavily, she leant back against the cracked wall. The sound of thunder merged with distant gunshots until a great silence fell over everything, as if a magic spell had robbed the world of sound.

Sellass looked up, searching for a sign that would forever seal her detachment from great sorrow. She felt deeply moved. In the sky, now clear of clouds, was a rainbow.

Epilogue

PUBLISHER'S NOTE: *The following letters are transcripts of the real letters between the person who inspired the character of Marianna and her correspondent.*

Milan, 20 November 1988

Dear Signor Carlo Cinzi,

For many years I have wanted to write to find out more about you but I never dared, for many reasons.

If I have decided to do so now, a decision which was not easy for me to make, it is to ask of you a favour, which I will explain below.

I wrote to the municipal offices of the town where you were born for your address and they instructed me to contact the Italian Consulate in South Africa, as you never returned to Italy.

Not long after doing so, I received your address from the Consulate. I knew the details of your place of birth because, when I was a child, I copied them down from a piece of paper that my mother kept hidden away, which was never found.

My name is Marianna, I was born in Massawa, and I have a brother called Gianfranco. My mother's name is Sellass. She made many sacrifices to raise my brother and me on her own. We lived in a poor neighbourhood on the outskirts of Asmara. Life for Italian-Eritrean children like us was very difficult, due to the poverty, loneliness and desperation. But I do not want to dwell on the many problems that we experienced or on the difficulty we had of blending in. I managed to find work in Addis Ababa when I was eighteen years old, and came to Italy a few years later. It took great strength and conviction to assimilate. I found a job, got married and then continued with my studies because I didn't want my children to have an uneducated mother. I have two daughters who bring me great joy: the older one is studying medicine, while the younger is finishing secondary school. I realise that I was lucky: my brother is in Asmara and life there is hard, but when hasn't it been? Eritrea has been at war for twenty-six years, and it is not easy to survive. They say that the Europeans are all leaving, that there is little work and a great deal of tension. The house that my mother managed to buy after years of working for an Italian family has been confiscated; she now lives in a rented room on the outskirts of Asmara. I receive news of her from a missionary priest who gave me precious advice over the years; I send him a little money each month to give to her. I have never wanted to go back. I went through many difficult years with my mother; she was poor, angry and deeply unhappy.

Signor Carlo, I am writing to ask if you would do something kind for her, as she is getting older now. If you would write her a letter and send it to Padre Gabriele, whose address I include, it would take a great burden off her heart. Please, I beg you, write to her and tell her why you left us, so that she understands. I'll never forget how she always used to ask herself the same question over and over: 'How could he...?' From my perspective, I have no recollection of ever seeing my mother feel joy, only deep grief and rage. And these images trouble my dreams to this day.

It is my hope that you will kindly fulfil my wish, for which I would be forever grateful.

With thanks and my most cordial wishes,

MARIANNA

Johannesburg, 4 January 1989

Dear Marianna,

I found your letter among some papers that belonged to my mother, Signora Martha Cinzi, who died last Friday after a long and painful illness. Carlo died last May, after having two heart attacks.

I do not know how helpful I can be, but your letter disturbed me greatly. I can't stop thinking about your words and about the woman you mention – Sellass. Who is she, Marianna?

I am Martha's daughter from her first marriage. I was ten years old when my mother got remarried to Carlo, whom she met here in Johannesburg. They had a son who died at the age of twenty. For Carlo it was like losing the light of his life; he adored that boy and soon afterwards started to experience long periods of depression.

I know that Carlo was held prisoner by the English in Massawa and taken to a prison camp in South Africa, where he was kept for five years. The ship carrying the prisoners to South Africa sank, and Carlo was one of only four men who survived, saved by the crew of another English ship. Carlo tried to escape from the camp twice but was captured both times. I know that this was a terrible experience for him, the conditions in the prison camp were awful. When the men got out, if they survived that long, they were battered and broken.

Carlo was an introvert but he often talked to me about certain periods in his life, how when he was twelve years old he went to America, and other things. But he never wanted to talk about his years in Eritrea. He refused. All he said was that it was terribly hot.

He was a kind, sad and devout man, he loved nature and animals, he spent long periods of time without speaking to anyone. Did Carlo have a painful secret?

I am so very sorry, Marianna, that your letter reached us too late, now that he is no longer with us.

I sincerely hope you will write back, so that I may learn more about you. We know very little about Carlo's Italian relatives. Occasionally he received letters from them, but he never returned to Italy.

With all best wishes,

ORIEL DOUGLAS

 **MUNKEN**

Learn more about the paper we use:

www.arcticpaper.com

Arctic Paper UK Ltd
8 St Thomas Street
London
SE1 9RS

Based on true events, this beautiful and moving story recounts a tale of love and betrayal in colonial Eritrea. At the outbreak of WWII, Sellass, an Eritrean young woman, and her two children are deserted by Carlo, an Italian young man who fathered Sellass' children. Now, rejected by both the local and Italian communities, Sellass needs to find a way to provide the bare essentials for her children, while taking her anger and frustration out on her daughter Marianna. As time goes by, Marianna will start wondering about her origins and start looking for her father.

Our edition includes the transcription of two real letters.

"*Abandonment recounts a universal if overlooked tale of empire: a young European man travels to the colonies in order to find opportunity and while there, falls in love and has children with a local woman whom he later abandons.*"

Erica L. Johnson, Pace University

£12.95

ISBN 978-1-7384594-0-7

www.heloisepress.com

Cover Design By Laura Kloos